Double Trouble

Second Edition

Double Trouble
Second Edition

Mike Faricy

Double Trouble: Second Edition © Copyright
Mike Faricy 2023

All rights reserved. No part of this publication may be reproduced, stored in a retrieval system, or transmitted, in any form or by any means, electronic, mechanical, photocopying, recording or otherwise, without the prior and express permission of the copyright owner.
    This is a work of fiction. All of the characters, organizations, and events portrayed in this novel are either products of the author's imagination or are used fictitiously.

Library of Congress Control Number: 2023914503
paperback ISBN: 978-1-962080-09-5
e-book ISBN: 978-1-962080-10-1

    MJF Publishing books may be purchased for education, Business, or promotional use. For information on bulk purchases, please contact the author directly at mikefaricyauthor@gmail.com

Published by

MJF Publishing
https://www.mikefaricybooks.com

To Teresa
"Oh for feck sake!"

Acknowledgments

I would like to thank the following people for their help and support:

Special thanks to my editors, Kitty, Donna and Rhonda for their hard work, cheerful patience and positive feedback.

I would like to thank Ann and Julie for their creative talent and not slitting their wrists or jumping off the high bridge when dealing with my Neanderthal computer capabilities.

Special thanks to Ann for her patience.

Last, I would like to thank family and friends for their encouragement and unqualified support. Special thanks to Maggie, Jed, Schatz, Pat, Av, Emily and Pat for not rolling their eyes, at least when I was there, and most of all, to my wife Teresa whose belief, support and inspiration has from day one, never waned.

Some years back...

I'd been living life dangerously for the better part of a month. Simultaneously dating the Flaherty sisters, Lissa and Candi, and all the while keeping our three-way relationship a secret from both of them. Their parents were out of town for the night, and Candi had returned home supposedly to keep an eye on her younger, fifteen-year-old brother, Tommy. We'd been doing tequila shots in her parents' basement rec room, and hadn't seen Tommy for hours. I learned later that he'd been hiding in the furnace room.

It was at the very peak of our passionate, tequila-fueled, midnight encounter. Blonde-haired Candi, wearing a hair ribbon and a smile, was on the virtual edge of incredible satisfaction, and so, in an effort to encourage, I whispered in her ear, "Oh, Lissa, Lissa, Lissa, you are so good."

Candi suddenly kicked me onto the tiled floor then screamed a number of incoherent expletives. Before I could make up an explanation, she staggered into the next room to get her father's hunting rifle. I decided it might be wise to exit, so I quickly pulled on my boxers and fled up the basement stairs carrying my jeans.

Other than their initial restraining orders, the threatening emails, and then Tommy's video, I hadn't heard from any of the Flaherty's in almost a decade…

One

It was my first day working collections for Andy Lindbergh. Things had slowed in the investigative world, so it was maybe a good thing I had the opportunity, maybe, but probably not. Andy had just shut down a six-month business brainstorm that turned out to be a business brain fart. He had eliminated the middle man, namely funeral parlors, allowing individuals to buy coffins directly from his company, theoretically at a substantial savings.

Two things happened; his existing mortician customers, his bread and butter, became really upset. And, Andy ended up getting stiffed, pardon the pun, intentionally or unintentionally by a number of individuals. He'd shut down the buy-direct operation and had put me on collections in an attempt to minimize losses.

There's something about calling folks for past due payments on coffins that can make for a long day. Not for the first time, I was on the line with a very nice, little old lady who probably still used a rotary dial phone.

"What was that you said?"

"I said I'm calling on behalf of Lindbergh Memorials regarding the past due amount on your account."

The coffin had apparently been for her husband. It wasn't like Andy had the option of digging it up and repossessing the thing, so a bit of finesse was needed. Was there even a market for a used coffin? I didn't think so.

"Clarence always dealt with those things, of course, he's passed on," she said, making it sound like he was out playing poker with the boys or just running to the hardware store.

"Yes, I'm sure he did, but there is a past due amount on your account, and I'd like to work with you to help bring your account current."

"Who did you say was calling?"

Things went downhill from there. At noon I walked into Andy's office. We'd been pals for years.

"How's it going?" he asked and attempted to look hopeful.

"Let me sum it up. I quit."

"Already?"

"Andy, I'm hassling octogenarians on social security regarding their monthly payment that is impossible for them to make. Even if they could hear me, they wouldn't understand what I'm talking about. I don't think I'm cut out for this."

"Maybe you're being too nice."

I placed a stack of files and an Excel spreadsheet on his desk.

"You got the wrong guy if you want me to play rough with these folks, I just can't do it."

"You know anyone who could?"

A name immediately popped into my head, but I debated mentioning him. "I know a guy who has dabbled in it a bit, collections that is. I have to be honest and tell you he did time a while back, maybe a year or two ago."

"Is he any good?"

"No, that's why he got caught."

"I meant with the collections."

"Oh, yeah, I think he's pretty good, at least as far as I know. Let me check him out, and I'll get back to you."

"Thanks for trying, Dev."

"Sorry, Andy, but I'm just not the guy."

Two

I'd known Tommy Flaherty since before I two-timed his older sisters, Candi and Lissa. Even as a young kid, Tommy had a reputation for getting into trouble coupled with an inability to realize consequences and an uncanny knack for always being the one who was going to get caught. Not the best of combinations.

He started his crime career early on in the primary grades stealing cafeteria lunch desserts. From there, he jumped to ripping off school lockers in junior high. He moved up to swiping cars in high school. Don't let me forget filming me with at least one of his sisters. Breaking and entering became his passion after senior year, for which he served twenty-four months up in the St. Cloud Reformatory.

Unfortunately, the St. Cloud stint only seemed to serve as a criminal finishing school, and upon completing that sentence, he graduated to armed robbery, whereupon he was once again arrested and this time served three-and-a-half years in Lino Lakes. At age twenty-four, he'd already spent close to a quarter of his life behind bars, which wasn't the most sterling point to have on one's résumé. The last I heard, Tommy had drifted into the collections area of the business world in an effort to go straight.

After I fled the basement all those years ago, Candi had phoned her sister Lissa in a drunken rage. The jig was up as the sisters quickly determined I had been dating them simultaneously. They threatened me with castration, filed restraining orders, and then promised further legal action if I ever attempted to contact them again.

I figured after a decade had passed, and since I was attempting to help their younger brother, I had at least a fighting chance. Well, and then there was the little matter of Tommy's video, which I never pursued.

"Hi, Candi, please."

"Speaking," she said. I could feel the chill through the phone.

"Candi, this is Dev Haskell. I…hello. Hello?"

I decided a slightly different tack might work with Lissa.

"Hello."

"Hi, Lissa, please don't hang up. I'm trying to reach your brother, Tommy. I have a job opportunity for him, but I don't have a phone number."

"Who the hell is this?"

"Please, don't hang up. It's Dev Haskell."

"Oh, hi, Dev. Long time no talk. How are you?"

"Lissa, I'm the dullest guy in town."

"I don't believe that for one minute."

"How have you been, Lissa?"

"Well, my sister's talking to me again, if that's your question."

"Actually, Candi just hung up on me, not more than ten minutes ago. I called her for Tommy's phone number, but as soon as I mentioned my name, she hung up."

"You really can't blame her, Dev. Calling out my name at a rather intimate moment wasn't the most romantic thing to do, and well, if you'll recall, it was all caught on film."

"Yes, and if I recall, the three of you made a tidy little profit selling that online."

"You have to admit it was classic. What on earth were you thinking, calling her by my name at that most inopportune of moments?"

"That was only because you were so good."

"She was in therapy for a couple of years after dating you."

"Well, you two girls and your little brother selling that video online didn't help matters."

"He's always had a bit of an entrepreneurial streak."

"Hiding in the basement and secretly filming us suggests a bit of a warped entrepreneurial perspective, don't you think?"

"Tommy's always been the creative type. Besides, a naked woman swearing at you with a hunting rifle was kind of funny. At least all the YouTube folks seemed to think so."

I thought it best not to go down that road. "Would you happen to have Tommy's phone number?"

"I have to ask why. No offense, but is this something legitimate? Or, is it another half-baked scheme you've cooked up? I hope you're not thinking of revenge. You weren't exactly lily-white on that whole deal, Dev. That's really the last thing anyone needs right now, Tommy's been straight for almost a year, and Candi's finally been able to get off those meds."

"Actually, that's why I'm calling. I heard he was doing collections. I've got a friend who's looking for someone, and I thought of Tommy."

"Is it legitimate?"

"Very, this guy is a straight arrow. You can check him out. The company is C. Lindbergh Memorials. My pal is Andy Lindbergh, he's the president, third generation. They do headstones, coffins, and just about anything you can think of in that industry. The thing is, there isn't much romance to it, but it could be a source of guaranteed employment for someone like your brother for, well, forever."

"He was doing collections up until recently, student loans. Of course, the problem is how are you going to collect from people who don't have any money, to begin with? He's been looking for something else, so from that standpoint, your timing couldn't be better."

"Great, I think he and Andy would really hit it off. Can you give me his number?"

"Why don't you give me yours and I'll have him call you."

"Okay, the sooner, the better," I said and gave her my number.

"Great talking, Dev. We should get together, just for old times' sake."

"Yeah, I'd like that, Lissa."

"I'd *really* like it," she said.

Three

Tommy called me the very next day. I'd already forgotten about trying to reach him and was sitting in my office, hoping the phone would ring with business. Tommy Flaherty wasn't exactly who I hoped to hear from.

"Haskell Investigations."

"Yeah, I'm looking for the video star that slept with both my sisters." That pretty much narrowed it down, but the accusation caught me off guard, and I had to pause for a half-second.

"Dev?"

"Yeah, Tommy?"

"Hey, didn't mean to scare you, man."

"Nice to hear from you, Tommy. How are things going?"

"Well, I've been out of the video biz for quite a while."

I didn't respond.

"Actually, thanks for asking, things couldn't be better."

In retrospect, from this point forward, I don't think anything Tommy told me was true.

"Here's the deal, Tommy, I got a pal who needs help with past due accounts." I went on to give him a brief rundown on what, exactly, Andy wanted. Then, I finished up with, "I'll be honest. I tried it and didn't last half a day. I'm just not cut out for collections."

"Most folks aren't, Dev. You've got to really want to help people, not that you don't, but I've been there, between a rock and a hard place. A lot of patience and a little luck can get you on the right track. I'd like to meet your guy, like to see you, too. We should get together, maybe grab a bite sometime."

"Yeah, sure, Tommy, we should do that."

"How about today? Say, maybe one-thirty. You free, man?"

"Free? Today? Well, yeah, I guess, I suppose I can do that. You pick the place, Tommy."

"You know the Over Easy? It's down on East Seventh."

I did know it. It was a twenty-four/seven joint that specialized in a cardiac arrest menu and girls to go. They'd been shut down by the health department for a week at the beginning of summer, and there'd been a shooting in the ladies' room sometime earlier this month.

"The Over Easy?"

"Yeah, it's just across from Doctor Romance."

Perfect. The sex toy store. You could work up an appetite with battery-operated friends then drift into the Over Easy for a heart-stopping meal.

"One-thirty, yeah, I guess that'll work, looking forward to seeing you again, Tommy."

The Over Easy was actually two old train cars pushed together to form a restaurant. The place was featured in postcards from the 1930s and had pretty much been on a downward slide ever since. I was sitting in a back booth waiting for Tommy, watching the collection of characters and smelling hot griddle grease for the better part of a half-hour. The tabletop and the red vinyl booth seemed to glisten from a patina of cooking oil.

Tommy pulled into a parking place across the street. He was driving a faded red, two-door Datsun sedan with a buckled hood and a tied down trunk. Or, was the dangling bumper tied up to the trunk? It was hard to tell.

He climbed out of the car, stared at the parking meter with the red flag showing time had expired, shook his head, muttered something, then crossed the street against traffic carrying what looked like a paper lunch bag.

"Hey, Tommy," some tattooed guy behind the counter called, then went back to filling coffee cups.

Tommy responded with a nod as he scanned down the length of booths looking for me.

I waved.

"Dev, nice to see you. Man, it's been a while," he said, sliding into the side opposite me. He needed a shave, and he looked like he'd slept in his clothes.

"Good to see you, Tommy, been a couple of years."

"Yeah, I suppose you heard I had a little vacation, compliments of the system," he said.

I felt like asking, "Which time?" Instead, I just nodded and glanced at the menu. "I appreciate you getting back to me so fast, Tommy. This company, there's no romance to the product line, unless you're maybe a vampire or something."

Tommy looked at me straight-faced and didn't blink.

"It's everything you can think of for the funeral biz," I said, then went on to explain Andy's business and what he needed.

"Sounds like just what I'm looking for, stable, with a future. God, my last gig was student loans, and I was working on commission. I think I only had a four percent success rate, and I was their top guy."

"So here's the contact information," I said, sliding an envelope across the table. Tommy glanced at the envelope then quickly slipped it into his pocket without opening it. I sensed a number of heads watching us and probably coming up with all sorts of weird scenarios.

He dove into breakfast, about five pounds' worth of greasy hash browns, greasy bacon, two greasy fried eggs, and something resembling hollandaise sauce slopped over the entire platter. After a few minutes, I'd pushed my platter to the side, but Tommy continued to diligently work his way through his.

"You gonna just let all that go to waste?" he said once he finished, then nodded at my heart-stopping order.

"Help yourself, if you've got the courage."

Once he cleaned my plate, he sat back with a satisfied smile. Maybe a minute or two later he picked up his brown paper lunch bag and said, "Would you excuse me for just a moment." He slid out of the booth and headed for the restroom.

He was gone for a good fifteen minutes. I wasn't surprised. The food at the Over Easy probably had that effect on most people. It was one of the reasons I'd pushed mine to the side. When he returned to the booth, he looked clean-shaven.

"Did you just shave in there?"

"Yeah, didn't Lissa mention it? You might say I'm highly mobile, right now."

"Highly mobile?"

"Kind of living in my car, you know, just until I get back on my feet. Shouldn't be too long, well, if this pans out, I hope. And I'm sure it will," he said, looking up at me, trying to sound positive.

"Your car?" I asked and looked out across the street at the buckled hood and the Bungee Cord holding things together in the rear.

"Couldn't you move in with Candi or Lissa? You know, just till you got back on your feet?"

"That really didn't work out too well with either one of them. They thought some things were missing, they never really said anything, but I know they blamed me. I just figured it would probably be better for all of us if I was on my own. Be great to have a place to land. You know, for maybe a day or so, couple of days, tops, just to tide me over until I got this job. And I'm gonna get it. I can feel it, Dev."

If I was supposed to respond, I didn't.

"Well, I suppose I should get going. I'll call your pal right away, soon as I find a payphone. I think there's one a couple of blocks over, maybe."

"You don't have a phone?"

"That's one of the first things I intend to address just as soon as I can. Well, that and I wanted to give some flowers to my Mom. I know, crazy, but it's just something I gotta do. She just loves flowers."

"I thought she passed away a couple of years back?"

"Oh yeah, she did," Tommy said, not meeting my eye. "I just wanted to leave them on her grave, you know make it look nice and all. She was such a wonderful woman."

"Isn't she buried back in Ohio, in a family cemetery or something?"

"That's why it's so expensive. I'd have to send them. You know, like Joe DiMaggio did for Marilyn Monroe."

I was beginning to wonder about the wisdom of passing Tommy Flaherty on to Andy.

Tommy picked up the tab and looked at it for a long moment. "You mind if we split this? I just have a C-note, and I was hoping I wouldn't have to break it."

"Let me get it, Tommy. My pleasure, besides, it was nice to see you again."

"You sure? I mean, I think I can cover my half. If that's what you want to do."

"No, my pleasure. Why don't you give me a call once you talk to Andy? Let me know how things went."

"Yeah, I'd be happy to, Dev. Hey, thanks again, I've been a little on the short side lately."

"Glad I could help, Tommy, talk to you later."

Four

Andy phoned me that afternoon. I was just about to head over to The Spot and meet my office-mate, Louie, for just one.

"Hey, Andy, how are things?"

"Great, spoke with your guy Flaherty this afternoon."

"Yeah, how'd it go?"

"Sounds like a really nice guy, polite, well-spoken. The last thing I need is some thug making calls. He's coming in tomorrow, but unless he crashes into my car in the parking lot, I'd say he's got the job."

I wasn't sure if I should offer congratulations or a warning. I decided to go positive. "That's great, Andy. I'm sure he'll work out and hopefully ease that list of past dues you're carrying."

"That's my hope, too. Well, I just wanted to say thanks."

"No, Andy, thank you for being a good guy and giving him a chance."

"Later," he said and hung up.

I walked over to The Spot. Louie was sitting four stools in from the front door. I signaled Jimmy for a round.

"You're certainly cheery for having accomplished absolutely nothing all day, again," Louie said.

"I'll have you know I did accomplish something today, and I'm pretty damn proud of it."

"Do tell," he said then nodded thanks to Jimmy as he slid my beer and Louie's next drink across the bar.

I proceeded to tell him my Tommy tale. How the guy was down and out just fighting for a second chance and coincidently I went the extra mile, was able to get in touch with him and give him Andy's number.

"And, I just got off the phone with Andy. He said he was going to offer Tommy the job."

"Well, you better watch it, much more of this behavior, and you'll be confusing all of us who have you pegged as a complete and utter asshole," Louie said then raised his fresh drink to me in a toast.

"Sorry to disappoint," I said.

We toasted one another for the better part of the evening, and I ended up taking the backstreets home. I pulled into my driveway, locked my car, and was halfway to the front door when a voice called my name.

"Dev?"

I jumped a couple of feet, looked around, and there was Tommy stepping out of the shadows. "Tommy, God, you scared the hell out of me, what's up?"

"I just wanted to tell you thanks again. I phoned Andy Lindbergh this afternoon. I think it went pretty well and I have an appointment with him tomorrow. Can't thank you enough for all you've done, man."

"My pleasure, Tommy."

He nodded like that seemed logical, then just stood there looking like the new kid in the neighborhood, hoping someone would pick him for their team.

I waited for a long, pregnant pause, then asked, "You got a place to stay tonight?"

"My car, I was gonna park on one of the side streets down by the police station. It's pretty safe down there, most of the time, usually."

"Look, I got a spare couch. Why don't you come on in and get a decent night's sleep, shower, and shave tomorrow morning, so you're on your best foot going in to talk with Andy."

"That's awfully nice of you, Dev. You sure I wouldn't be cramping your style?"

"Tommy, it's after two in the morning, and I didn't bring anyone home. I don't have a lot going on right now, so grab your stuff and come on in."

"I'm traveling light," he said and followed me up the steps.

I showed him where the guest bath was and got him a glass of water. "If you're the first one up tomorrow, this is how you make the coffee," I said, pouring water into the coffee maker then scooping six spoonfuls of grounds into the filter. "See that button at the base of the coffee pot?"

"Yeah."

"All you gotta do is push that thing."

"I think I can remember that."

"What time are you meeting Andy tomorrow?"

"Eleven, I'm praying I'll be walking out of there with a job."

"Just be yourself, Tommy. Who wouldn't want to hire you?"

Five

Tommy was gone by the time I got up, but then again, it was almost noon. The coffee was still on with maybe a half-cup left in the pot. I just hoped all went well for both him and, more importantly, Andy.

"Just calling to say thanks, again," Andy said when he called a little after four.

"You hired him?"

"Yeah, in fact right now he's working at the same desk where you failed so miserably, he's been making collection calls since noon. No offense, but he's already done about a thousand percent better than you."

"Terrific."

"Yeah, he wanted to work until eight tonight, said you actually get the best results between six and eight. Which I guess maybe makes sense."

"He'd know better than me."

"Or me. Anyway, I just wanted to thank you again, Dev. He's gonna be a great addition. I'm thinking, there are all sorts of possibilities for someone with his talents."

"Glad to hear it, Andy, and thanks for giving him a chance."

"Your guy get the job?" Louie asked, looking up from the picnic table that served as his desk.

"Not only did he get it, but he's working there right now. Andy says he's already making an impact and wants to work until about eight tonight, says between six and eight is the best time to connect with folks for collections. Andy's thrilled."

"Great, so it's a win all around?"

"Yeah, you know every once in a while, I guess you can do something nice for someone, and it doesn't come back and bite you in the ass."

We wandered over to The Spot for a few hours to celebrate Tommy's success. When I pulled into my driveway later that night, Tommy was standing on the front porch. It looked like he was just knocking on the door.

"So?" I said, climbing the front steps.

"Oh hi, Dev, didn't realize you weren't home. Hey, I got the job. Actually, I worked until eight tonight, really a nice guy."

"Well, I gotta tell you, I got a call from him this afternoon, and he's pretty damn happy. You'll be a great addition there, Tommy."

"I can't thank you enough for the help, all the advice, putting me in touch with Andy and, of course, the place to stay last night."

"My pleasure, Tommy. What are your plans for tonight?"

"Tonight?"

"That pretty much answers my question. You want to flake out on my couch again?"

"Would you mind? I have to be at work tomorrow, by ten. God, it feels great having a job to go to."

"Come on in," I said, then slipped my key in the lock. My front door was unlocked, and I figured I must have forgotten to lock the door on my way out that morning, which was very unusual for me.

I was going to throw some cold pizza in the microwave, but there wasn't any in the fridge, so I ordered another. Tommy had a piece when it arrived but didn't seem that hungry. He flaked out on the couch while I had another beer. I was going to make coffee for the morning, but it was already made. I figured I was losing my mind if I couldn't remember making it, and the best thing to do was just go to bed.

I spent the following day checking references and employment details on about a hundred job applications for a client. Then, I called Heidi to see about a night of debauchery.

"Hi, Heidi, you got any plans for tonight?"

"Nothing that can't be postponed if the right offer comes across."

"I would be happy to bring dinner over, or if you feel like it, I could wine and dine you at some intimate little place."

"What's this going to cost me?"

"Cost you? Nothing. You won't have to pay a cent."

"I wasn't talking money, Dev."

"Well, I don't know, I suppose we could see how the night goes and maybe…."

"I was kidding, dopey. It's just nice to hear you grovel."

"If it wasn't so good, I wouldn't have made this call in the first place. Believe me, you're good, and I'm groveling."

"Pick me up at seven and you choose the place, but please, let's go somewhere nice this time. Not those usual greasy spoon dives you go to for cheeseburgers and beer. Pick someplace romantic."

"We could do dinner in bed."

"I'll see you at seven, and don't be late."

I was at Heidi's at 7:15. She wasn't ready. We ended up at a quiet little Italian restaurant over on University forty minutes later. Despite the sheet of plywood covering the broken glass in the front door, it had the feel of a family place, and apparently tonight, the family wasn't talking. The wife served as hostess, and her husband was our waiter. They were both pleasant enough when dealing with us, but when they were away from the table, we could hear them arguing in the kitchen.

"I wonder what he did," Heidi said.

"I heard it on the news the other night, someone stole their ATM machine, hauled it right out of the place. That's why there's plywood over the front door."

"Then I don't blame her for being unhappy," Heidi said and sipped.

I weighed my options, thought about the potential for the rest of the night. "You're absolutely right."

She looked at me for a long moment and said, "That was sweet, Dev."

Despite the bickering emanating from the restaurant kitchen, we had a pleasant meal. On the way home, Heidi had that warm glow she gets when she's very content and has been a little overserved. "Want to come in for a glass of wine and stay for breakfast?" she asked as we pulled up in front of her place.

"I think that sounds like a great idea." I spent the night and woke up just long enough to hear Heidi tell me thanks before she flew out the door, then I rolled over and drifted back to sleep.

I went home to shower and change. Something didn't seem right the moment I stepped in the door. I couldn't quite put my finger on it, and then I realized I smelled coffee. The pot was empty, the kitchen looked like I'd left it, but I was sure I smelled coffee. I felt the pot, it wasn't warm, or was it? I opened the top, and there wasn't a filter or grounds in there, but there was moisture. I wasn't sure, maybe it was just from the day before.

I checked the dishwasher, there were more mugs than usual, but then again, Tommy had spent two nights here, so that made sense. Was the shower wet? I'd already turned it on when I noticed water on the glass, maybe, I couldn't really tell. I wondered if I was becoming paranoid.

I had to deliver my results on all the employment references to my client later in the afternoon, and I wanted to wear something more than a t-shirt. I pulled on some decent slacks, a clean golf shirt, but couldn't find the sport coat I was looking for and wondered if I'd left it at someone's house. Once again, the thought of losing what was left of my mind bounced around in my thick skull.

Six

A couple of days later, I was at my desk scanning the apartment building across the street through my binoculars. One of the girls in the third-floor unit had been running back and forth from the kitchen to a bedroom wearing just a towel around her head. I sat waiting patiently for her next appearance when the phone rang.

"Haskell Investigations," I said, holding the phone with my left hand and the binoculars with my right.

"Dev, Heidi."

"Everything all right?"

"Yeah, I'm looking for a date, you busy tonight?"

"I'm sure I'll be able to deliver whatever particular perversion you're in the mood for."

"Not what I meant, you perv. I have to go to a fundraiser tonight. A client sent me tickets. I just need someone on my arm. I had one of my girlfriends lined up, but she canceled."

"Let me guess, that Mary Francis person."

"How did you know?"

"Because she always cancels. Yeah, I can go with you. What time do you want me to pick you up?"

"Is six okay?"

"I'll be there," I said and went back to scanning across the street.

Heidi's fundraising events were quasi-formal things that collected a higher class of criminal than the ones I usually rubbed shoulders with. These were big-time scammers; lawyers, politicians, bankers, and business owners. The hors d'oeuvres would be lousy and too few, with lite beer that was warm and overpriced, watered-down drinks that were too expensive. Heidi usually made it worth my while at the end of the night.

I rang her doorbell right on time. After the third ring Heidi answered the door in her bathrobe.

"Don't say anything. I'm almost ready, just give me a moment. Go pour yourself a beer in the kitchen."

I did as commanded, then sat on a kitchen stool and sipped.

"Just be a minute," she called about fifteen minutes later. I'd been here before, many times before. I figured since the hors d'oeuvres were bound to be lousy, I'd search her cupboards. I came up with rice cakes and an opened bag of lime-flavored Dorito chips that were so stale they didn't crunch when I bit into one. I ate them anyway.

"Almost ready," she said after maybe another five minutes. The chips were gone, and the beer was empty. I debated opening another.

"Just going to pee, and then we'll go," she called sometime after that. I should have opened that second beer ten minutes earlier. I heard the toilet flush, then the sink running, then something spray or spritz. She walked into the kitchen and looked at me while she attached an earring. "That's what you're wearing?"

"I suppose I could run home and change."

She actually seemed to think about that option for a moment then said, "No, we're already late. Do you have a tie in the car?"

"I'm not wearing a tie."

She shook her head then picked up a purse and keys. The purse was small, a little fancy white beaded thing. It looked like it would barely hold a couple of credit cards, and I wondered how that was going to work.

"Here, just carry these for me," she said, then handed me a comb, a hair brush with a folding handle, lipstick, an eyebrow pencil, some makeup compact thing, and a small perfume bottle.

"What do you want me to do with all this?"

"Just bring it and don't complain," she said.

I headed to the car as she locked the front door.

"We better take my car. No telling what people would think if we arrived in that bomb of yours."

I was driving a silver Sebring, no whitewalls, with a trunk that was sprayed flat black. I'd gotten a great deal on it at the police auction.

"You want me to drive your car?"

"Yeah, I've got some touch up to do," she said, then stood next to the passenger door of her BMW and waited for me to open it for her. I watched her get in, then dumped all the things I was supposed to carry in her lap and closed the door.

She had the mirror on the sun visor down before I climbed behind the wheel.

"Heidi, you look wonderful, you always do, just relax and enjoy the ride."

"Just a little touch," she said, doing something to her eye with a pencil. "Where'd you get that coat?" she asked, referring to my black and white checked sport coat.

"Like it?"

"Not really."

"I got it at Sonny's."

"The bargain rack? I'm amazed they even let you out of the store with that thing."

"I think it looks great."

"The collar tab on your shirt is unbuttoned."

"Yeah, the button must have come off at the dry cleaners."

"Or, when it was lying on your bedroom floor for a week."

"Are we going to be happy by the time we get there?"

"Okay, here's the deal, I think a potential client is going to be here, and maybe I'm just a little nervous. I've been working on this guy for over a year."

"A little nervous, you've been bitching since you let me in the door. Anything I can do to help?"

"Yes, escort me in the door, then stay away. I'll signal if I need anything."

"Sounds fun."

"It's business for me, Dev. You'll get your reward at the end of the night, provided you behave."

"I promise to be good," I said.

Seven

The valet opened the door for Heidi, then just stood there and stared with his mouth half-open as she climbed out of the car.

"Do I get a receipt?" I asked, bringing him back to reality.

"Huh? Oh, yes sir, here you go," he said then went back to staring at Heidi as she walked into the hotel. Signs for the fundraiser pointed in the direction of an escalator that carried us up to the second floor.

"I'll just be a minute," Heidi said as we stepped off the escalator, and she made a beeline for the ladies' room.

"Can I get you something?"

"A white wine would be nice," she called over her shoulder. I watched a half dozen heads turn as she made her way down the broad foyer.

I waited in line at the bar for Heidi's white wine and a lite beer for me. Both items were over priced, the beer was warm, and I noticed the tip jar was definitely looking on the sparse side. I carried the drinks back and waited a discreet distance from the ladies' room with a half dozen other guys. Heidi returned about fifteen minutes later.

"God, this wine isn't even chilled, you should have gotten an ice cube to put in it."

"At least yours was cold when I got it."

"Sorry, I'm just a little nervous, this could be a big account for me, real big."

"Well, you're the best looking woman here, and if he doesn't go for you, then you don't want to work with him because the guy would be an idiot."

"Thanks, but this isn't about boobs, Dev, it's about business and being professional. Still, you know in your own silly, chauvinistic way you're kind of nice, I think…."

"Heidi? Heidi Bauer, is that really you?"

"Why, Royal," she called to some fat guy then left me in the dust as she strutted toward him.

I wandered off into the crowd but kept Heidi in sight from time to time just in case she needed anything.

"Pardon me, sir, but I think you're in the wrong place, the strippers are next door," a voice said from behind.

I turned around, and there was Andy. "Hey, Andy, didn't figure you for this stuff. I hope you're passing out cards, some of these guys look like they could drop over from a heart attack at any minute."

"God, if only it was that easy," he laughed then took a sip from his wine glass. "Hey, you must have gotten that coat from Tommy, he wore one just like it when I interviewed him the other day."

"Great minds think alike. Is he still working out?"

"Yeah, what a tiger, the guy just wants to work. He's there right now going till eight again tonight. And, he's getting results for me, too."

"Really, that's great."

"Yeah, can't thank you enough, Dev. Hey, that's my wife over there looking for me, I better get moving. Thanks again. Enjoy your night."

"You too, Andy, and behave."

I lingered around one of the portable bars, delivered another glass of wine to Heidi then made myself scarce. I was right, the few remaining hors d'oeuvres were lousy. Teams of people were walking through the crowd selling raffle tickets at a hundred bucks a pop for two, round trip, first-class tickets to anywhere in the world. I couldn't remember winning anything like that in my life, and I figured at a hundred bucks a pop this wasn't the place to try and start.

From across the room, Heidi raised her eyebrows, then her glass, signaling for another wine. I came past as discreetly as possible and handed her the wine, trying not to interrupt her conversation.

"Oh, thanks, Dev. Royal, this is the fellow I mentioned earlier, Dev Haskell, he's a private investigator."

"Hi, Royal Baker, nice to meet you," he said and held out his hand. He was maybe an inch shorter than me, close to a hundred pounds heavier with thinning brown hair and a ruddy complexion.

"Dev Haskell, Royal, very nice to meet you."

"Heidi was telling me you're a private investigator."

"That's right."

"I'd like to talk to you. I have a situation at work, but for a number of reasons I'd like to keep it very private and not have law enforcement involved, at least until I know for sure what we're dealing with."

"Be happy to talk with you. Would sometime this week work?"

"Could you fit me in tomorrow?" he said, then magically produced a business card.

I pulled my wallet out, flipped past a couple of dollar bills, a twenty, a grocery list, and my old expired driver's license before I found a business card and handed it to him. "I'll call you tomorrow," I said.

"I look forward to it."

Heidi gave me a "get lost" indication from behind Royal then smiled demurely, as he turned toward her.

"Well, if you'll excuse me. I've a client I have to catch up with, a pleasure meeting you. I'll call you tomorrow. Heidi, nice to see you," I said, then beat a hasty retreat to a distant bar.

Eight

Heidi took another giant gulp of wine and said, "I can't believe he wants you to call him tomorrow, God." She was curled into the corner of her living room couch. She'd kicked her heels off at the door, tossed her earrings on the coffee table, and began to unwind.

"Well, thanks for passing my name on. I don't even know what the guy does," I said and fished out his business card from my coat pocket. There were actually two cards in there, the one from Royal Baker and another from Andy. I didn't recall Andy ever giving me a card. Royal Baker's listed him as President and CEO of Tri-Cort Services, Limited.

"What the hell does Tri-Cort Services stand for?"

"I'm not exactly sure. It's some internet subscription service."

"You mean like a newspaper?"

"No, they're into more of a security kind of thing."

"Like guys in parking lots?"

"Yeah, that's what they do, Dev, they collect parking fees in parking lots. No, it's more like online security. He has a bunch of different web sites, I guess the things are all over the world, very successful. Anyway, it lets you conduct business anonymously or something."

"What are you trying to do with him?"

"The company is sitting on a pile of cash. They had a huge increase in cash balance in the first versus the fourth quarter last year, something like twenty-five percent of revenue. I've got some ideas on making that work and beating the taxman at the same time."

Before my eyes glazed over, I asked, "Is he going to go for it?"

"Well, he hasn't said no, yet. But I'd kill for the response you got tonight."

"Your work might be just a little more involved. He probably just wants me to make sure everyone has a current driver's license. He must be interested, Heidi, he spent a good part of the night talking to you. Well, unless he's making a play?"

"A play? For me? No, don't be stupid."

"It's a logical question, but if he's not, then wouldn't it stand to reason that he's interested in what you have to say, maybe listen to your opinion?"

"I suppose," she said and took a sip. I could see she was thinking.

"Were you talking mostly business, your usual finance and investment shit?"

"Yeah, we talked all business from that standpoint."

"And you talked to him for what, an hour? Longer?"

"I suppose."

"I'd say you just had your first appointment, it wasn't in his office, but he was sounding you out, and you were probably doing the same to him."

Heidi raised her near empty glass and smiled. "I think a refill is in order, and I could use a back rub," she said.

I gave her a look.

"Oh, God, just do it, and things are likely to go your way," she said, then took a healthy sip.

I called Royal Baker the following morning, about half-past ten. Heidi was still asleep with a smile on her face. I was at her kitchen counter on my second cup of coffee.

"And who may I say is calling?" the receptionist said.

"My name is Dev Haskell, I met with Mr. Baker last night, and he asked me to call him today."

"One moment, please."

Some highbrow symphony music flooded over the line for a couple of minutes. Then the receptionist came back on and said, "Thank you for waiting. I'll connect you now."

There were a couple of clicks, and then a woman answered. "Mr. Baker's office."

"My name is Dev Haskell. I'm calling for Mr. Baker."

"Mr. Baker is in a meeting right now. He wondered if you could meet him this afternoon at 1:30."

"I can do that."

"I'm putting you on his schedule, Mr. Haskell. My name is Marilynn. I'll alert the security desk that you'll be arriving early this afternoon. When you arrive, if you would please have them contact me, I'll escort you up to our office once you've received your visitor's badge."

"I'll see you this afternoon."

"Please be on time," she said and hung up.

I suppose I could have made breakfast, gotten dressed, and gone to my office or maybe gone home and showered. I weighed those options and thought it might be more promising to climb back in bed with Heidi.

An hour later, and Heidi was in one of her cuddly moods resting her head on my chest. We were relaxing in the afterglow.

"Say, don't forget to call Royal Baker today," she said, running her finger back and forth on my chest.

I was thinking there was a good chance there just might be another go-round with Heidi in my immediate future. "I already talked to him."

She stopped with her playful hand and sat up. "You did? When?"

"This morning, you were still asleep, and I didn't want to wake you."

"You didn't have any problem waking me up a little while ago."

"That was different. Besides, you didn't seem to mind."

"What did he say? Are you going to meet with him?"

"I've got a 1:30 appointment."

She looked at the digital on her makeup table. It was just past noon. "Get out of here," she said and started to push me out of bed.

"Relax, I'll grab a quick shower, and it's a ten-minute drive if I step on it."

"You're not going to see Royal Baker dressed in the same dreadful clothes you had on last night. Get out of this bed."

"Will you just relax?"

"No, I will not, get dressed, go home and get cleaned up. I don't want him thinking you were here last night, and we were fooling around until early afternoon."

"It might be just the thing to get you in the door."

"Get out," she screamed, then climbed out of bed and went into the bathroom. When she came back, I was still lying in bed.

She grabbed a white Terrycloth robe from the back of a chair and began pulling it on. "Dev, I'm not kidding. This is really important to me. I gave him your name. You have an appointment, now get the hell out of here and don't screw it up," she said cinching the robe tightly around her waist to make her point.

I got dressed and headed for her front door.

"Call me when you're finished, I want to hear all about it," she said then clicked the lock behind me before I was even off the front stoop.

Nine

I got cleaned up at home. I couldn't find the sport coat I had planned on wearing and so settled for a nice, conservative navy-blue blazer with brass buttons. I think it was the same style coat Peter Rabbit left on Mr. McGregor's fence.

Tri-Cort Services, Limited, was in a fairly new six-story building just off of I-94. I must have driven past the place a million times and never paid any attention. The building security desk was about fifteen feet inside the revolving door and situated in front of a wall mural that looked like a giant wiring diagram. The floor was a buff-colored glazed stone so shiny you could almost see your reflection. You had to pass in front of the security desk to get to the elevators. I told them I had an appointment with Royal Baker, and I was to ask for Marilynn. I signed a roster, got issued a red and white visitor's badge that I hung around my neck and then waited patiently in a comfortable leather chair.

Marilynn arrived about five minutes later. She stepped off an elevator set just far enough away from the bank of five other elevators to suggest it was private. The other elevator doors were industrial brushed steel, but

Marilynn's elevator had brass doors embossed with a scene depicting trees and a sunset.

She took three steps off the elevator then stood in a perfect "meet the queen" pose with her hands clasped in front of her and her right foot set at a forty-five-degree angle behind the left. She wore an attractive, conservative suit, and her hair was nicely styled. She had a silver flower pin attached to her lapel, and she looked all business.

"Devlin Haskell," she called, and I felt like I had just been summoned to the principal's office.

"Yes," I said jumping up and hurrying toward her with my hand extended. "You must be Marilynn."

"Very nice to meet you, Mr. Haskell." She grasped my hand for half a second then made a grand gesture toward the private elevator.

"Please, after you," I said.

She smiled and led the way. Some soft violin music filled the elevator and seemed to immediately remove one from the chaos of the outside world. There were only two buttons. She pushed the one labeled "up" as the doors closed then half-turned to face me.

"Mr. Baker is on an extremely tight schedule. I've allotted fifteen minutes for him to discuss things with you. I'll knock on his office door in exactly fifteen minutes from your entry. Please don't think I'm needlessly interrupting. Unfortunately, he has quite a number of things to attend to today."

The doors opened, and I moved back a half step, indicating she should go ahead of me. We walked down a nicely paneled hallway on thick carpeting, leading toward a set of massive double doors. She input a six-digit code on the security lock. I heard a loud snap, and she pushed one of the large doors open.

We entered a round, spacious office with a large desk stationed in front of another set of double doors. A set of armchairs and a coffee table with neatly arranged magazines were positioned within glaring distance of the desk. Marilynn was clearly keeper of the gate.

"If you would wait just a moment, I'll see if you can go in," she said, then pushed a button on her desk phone and placed a white headset to her ear. "Yes, sir, I have Mr. Devlin Haskell to see you. Yes. Yes. Very good."

"He'll see you now, Mr. Haskell," she said, then put the headset down, grandly opened one of the doors behind her desk, and I entered the king's chambers.

Royal Baker sat behind a massive U-shaped desk positioned in the corner of his office so that he had windows to his left and right. Behind him was a hundred and eighty-degree view of treetops stretching all the way to the Mississippi River. He signaled me with an index finger indicating one. One of what, I wasn't quite sure of. After a moment, he put his pen down and tossed his glasses on the desk as he stood. I noticed a framed photo of him, and I guessed his wife on his desk. Royal had a wide grin pasted on his face, and the woman, a brunette with short hair, and apparently no makeup looked like a kid who had just been told to stand in the corner for another time out.

"Mr. Baker, nice to see you again."

"Please, let's keep it informal, Dev, call me Royal."

"Okay, Royal."

"Let's sit over here. We'll both be more comfortable," he said, indicating a leather couch and two matching armchairs against a wall. "Oh, man, I tell you, it never seems to end," he said, taking a seat on the couch.

I sat in one of the armchairs and nodded like I knew what he was talking about.

He tilted his head back and closed his eyes.

I waited for what seemed like a year until finally, I said, "You mentioned tht something was private you wished to talk about. I believe you said it was work-related, and you were hoping not to have law enforcement involved, at least initially."

He seemed to blink himself back to reality, then cleared his throat. "Here's my problem. One of our, or rather, my *very* special clients, is being harassed. I'd like you to find out who's doing it."

"Define harassed. Is someone spray painting the side of their building, picketing their office, or maybe sending threatening letters?"

"To tell you the truth, I wish that was the case. No, they've somehow bypassed our security systems and firewalls. Without boring you with the technical details, they're posting bad reviews, changing my client's profiles, and inserting different images."

"Reviews? Profiles? You make it sound like Facebook or something."

"Not far from the truth. If word of this got out, it could put us out of business, literally overnight. We deal with a series of websites that have a discrete online presence. We cater to a need for absolute client confidentiality."

"If this is some technical thing, Royal, you know with computers and stuff? Let me be honest. I'm probably not the guy."

"No, this client is local, and whoever the individual is harassing her, they're local as well. They seem to be behaving in such a way as to suggest they want us to know they're local. But, as I mentioned, if word of this got out, well, we would probably have to close the doors."

"So, that's why you don't want law enforcement involved?"

"Partially, right now, we're just trying to contain."

"Royal, just to be clear, I've got my passwords written down and stored on my Rolodex, literally. It sounds like you might need some high tech investigators. Pardon the stereotype, but shouldn't you be looking for a nerd?"

"I've already done that, brought them in from the outside, so they have no relation to any of our teams. Thus far, they haven't found a thing."

"If they're not finding anything, I'm not sure what it is that I can do for you."

"I was hoping maybe some old fashioned investigative work. If you could just meet with our client, I think that would go a long way in putting her at ease. Let her tell you what's been happening and take it from there. I've already drawn up a shortlist of disgruntled former employees I suspect could be involved, but to be honest, they're all long shots."

"It sounds like you're grasping at straws."

"I'd say right now that's a fairly accurate assessment."

The door opened, and Marilynn stepped in. "Mr. Baker, they're waiting for you in the conference room."

'Shit," he said under his breath. "Thank you, Marilynn. I'll be there in a moment. Dev, don't give me an answer right now, just promise me you'll think about it. Let me know in, oh, say, the next twenty-four hours. Fair enough?"

"That works for me. I'll get back to you tomorrow."

"Excellent. Marilynn will escort you back to the lobby."

"If you'll follow me, Mr. Haskell," Marilynn said then walked out of the office. I had to hurry to catch up.

Ten

We were sitting on our usual stools at The Spot, and it was Louie's turn to buy. "So, that's what he wants you to do, meet with his client?" Louie asked.

"Yeah, I guess. I don't know, the way he explained things, my first thought is it would be some nerd screwing things up on this woman's computer. He said he'd drawn up a list of disgruntled former employees. It's probably some brainy dipshit either hanging out at the library or home on his computer all night long listening to Star Wars music playing in the background."

"Good thing you're not stereotyping. Was this Royal guy purposely vague?" He signaled Mike, the bartender for another round.

"I don't know, it just seems to me, at least at first glance, whoever is doing this is smart. I'm just wondering if they're smart enough not to be involved."

"You're not making any sense. Maybe I should just cancel that next beer for you?"

"Don't. What I mean is Royal is thinking its some local disgruntled computer hack. God, it's probably just some high school kid acting stupid and getting his kicks."

Mike slid my beer, and Louie's bourbon across the bar then took a ten from our pile of cash.

"So, are you going to take the job?" Louie asked.

"Sounds like I would be getting paid just to follow people around and see if anyone is into anything crazy."

"Sounds like a waste of time," Louie said and sipped.

"Probably, but now I'd be getting paid for wasting it."

"There you go, always looking at the bright side."

"That's me. God, I don't even know what to look for. I'm still thinking this is way out of my league."

"Maybe wait until you talk to his client, the one being harassed. In the meantime, what about that professor that always helped you with computer stuff, well, until you downloaded all that porn on her laptop?"

"You mean, Sunnie Einer. And I didn't do that intentionally. I don't know, it just happened. Which is the perfect example of me not being a tech guy."

"Gee, really, who knew?"

"I don't know, this could get awfully complicated, and I haven't even been involved yet."

"Sounds to me like you're already signed on."

Eleven

I phoned Royal during lunch the following day. I was at my desk eating a Stromboli while I scanned the building across the street with my binoculars. I was having better luck with the Stromboli.

"Mr. Baker's office."

"Hi, this is Dev Haskell. Is this Marilynn?"

"Yes, Mr. Haskell, how may I help you?"

"I'd like to speak to Royal, please."

"Mr. Baker is in a meeting just now, may I have him call you."

"Yes, I think that will work, I've got a number of meetings this afternoon, but I'll leave word to be interrupted when he calls," I said, then decided that sounded like a pretty good line and took a large bite of the Stromboli.

"Very well, your number, please," Marilynn said.

I attempted to push the Stromboli to one side of my mouth and almost choked, trying to give her my number.

"I'm sorry, I'm having difficulty understanding what you said. Would you mind repeating that, please?"

I took a big swallow and repeated my number.

"There, much better. Thank you, I'll have Mr. Baker get in touch with you. Will there be anything else?"

"No, that should do it. I'll alert my staff that he's going to be calling."

"Yes, I'm sure you will," she said, sounding like she didn't believe a word then hung up.

Royal called back late in the afternoon. I was debating about going home or drifting over to The Spot.

"Haskell Investigations."

"Mr. Haskell, please."

"Royal?"

"Oh, Dev. I didn't realize this was your private line."

"Nothing's too good for you, Royal, thanks for calling back. I'd like to take on this harassment situation we discussed yesterday."

"Wonderful, let me phone Ashley right now and let her know you're going to be involved."

"Ashley," I said, writing her name down. "And what's her last name?"

"Ashley should do."

"What's her number?"

"I'll have her contact you. We're all a bit security conscious right now. Glad you're on the case, Dev."

"I look forward to talking with her," I said, but he'd already hung up, not the most promising of beginnings.

Ashley phoned me later that evening. I was still in The Spot watching the Twins get their asses handed to them when she called.

"Haskell Investigations," I answered then watched as we hit into a bases-loaded double play to close out the third inning. We were already down four to zip.

"Devlin Haskell, please." A sultry voice that sounded more than a little like Marilyn Monroe melted my cellphone.

"Speaking, how can I help you?"

"This is Ashley."

"Oh, yeah, Ashley. Hey, thanks for calling back. I spoke with Mr. Baker, and he briefly described your situation. I was hoping we might be able to get together and discuss some things."

"Mmm-hmmm, I'd like that."

Based on her voice, I thought I might, too. "Is there a time that would work for you tomorrow?"

"I might be able to meet later in the afternoon. I've got an appointment in an hour, and it's liable to go pretty late."

An appointment? At this hour? It must be some international conference call or something. "I think I can adjust my schedule, move some people around. Does four tomorrow afternoon work? I could come to your office if that would be more convenient."

"I'd prefer to meet in some public place."

"Okay," I said, thinking 'strange,' but maybe she'd already checked me out and wasn't so sure. "Just tell me where and I'll meet you there."

"I have to pick up some things tomorrow, how about the Mall of America, there's a Starbucks on the second floor, just around the corner from Victoria's Secret. Do you know it?"

"Yes," I lied. I avoided the Mall of America like the plague. My blood pressure rose, just driving past the damn place. Store after store and not one with anything I wanted or needed. I'd lost count of the number of women who had dragged me out there for "just a moment," only to be abandoned for hours while they wandered aimlessly without the slightest idea of what they were looking for, delighted just to be shopping.

"Wonderful, please don't be late, I'm on a tight schedule," she said and hung up.

I wondered how tight her schedule could be if she was out at The Mall in the first place? Fortunately, she'd hung up before I could ask.

Twelve

I was sitting in the second floor Starbucks out at The Mall the following afternoon, ten minutes ahead of schedule, not that it mattered, Ashley didn't show for another forty-five minutes. When she did arrive, she had three bright pink shopping bags from Victoria's Secret, a black bag with gold lettering from Sheba's, another lingerie store, two other bags I couldn't identify, a bag from Nordstrom's holding two shoeboxes and a purse slung over her shoulder large enough to carry a rocket launcher.

I had been staring at her from across the room as she ordered a latte with skim milk and artificial sweetener. At the time I didn't know it was Ashley, I just sat there treading water and letting the slutty ambiance she seemed to exude wash over me. I don't know if it was the long blonde hair, the incredibly tight leopard skin stretch pants, the see-through top, her black stiletto heels with the little spurs, the breast enhancement, or the cloud of perfume wafting from three tables over. I'd already chalked her up as probably being too much work.

Once she got her latte, she looked around at everyone staring at her, then walked toward my table. "You must be Dev," she cooed in that Marilyn Monroe voice as she set her mug on the table. She proceeded to unload the half dozen bags she carried and scatter them around my stool. Then she held out a hand with long, red fingernails and a rose with thorns tattooed around her wrist. As I took her hand, she automatically stroked my palm with her middle finger, raised an eyebrow suggestively, and batted her long, fake eyelashes.

I started to pant and suddenly felt my blood pressure rise, which had nothing to do with being in the Mall of America.

"Nice to meet you, Ashley. I wasn't sure that was you at the counter."

"It's all me," she shrugged and wrinkled her nose.

Everyone in the place was trying very hard not to look like they were staring at her.

"Yeah, well, Mr. Baker gave me just the briefest information. You apparently have a problem with someone posting things on the internet, your profile, or something?"

"Yeah, someone's been following me, taking pictures then posting them on my business profile. There was a photo of me working out, another one at my yoga class, jogging, then a couple of shots coming out of," she seemed to think for a moment, "business meetings."

"All taken locally?"

She nodded while sipping. "Yeah, from all over town. After the first couple of images were posted, I started to watch, but I could never spot anyone taking my picture."

"Maybe they're using a long-range lens," I said, thinking out loud.

"That's the same thing Royal said, but the workout and yoga shots were in fairly close quarters. In fact, the yoga room doesn't even have windows."

"And why are they doing this, do you know?"

"I think they're just screwing with me," she said, then shrugged and sipped her latte. The two women at the table next to us stared at one another with shocked expressions.

"But, whoever it is, seems to be able to post whatever and whenever they want on my profile page. It's supposed to be secure, but obviously, it's not. Roy has already shut down my site twice, and I've had to fill in all the information again for a new site. Let me tell you, not fun."

"Roy? You mean, Mr. Baker, Royal?"

"Yeah, sometimes I call him Roy," she wrinkled her nose and shrugged again. "He kinda likes that, he takes good care of me, tells me I'm special. Well anyway, we've changed my password more times than I can remember, but that didn't do anything. He even bought me a new computer, but that didn't seem to help, either."

This was sounding more and more like it was out of my technical skill range. I was quickly becoming convinced I was probably the wrong guy for the job. "What kind of business are you in?"

She looked more than a little surprised. "Are you kidding? Why I'm an escort, of course. You pay, and I'll play," she said, then wrinkled her nose at me. "What did you think? Why the hell else would I be dealing with Roy?"

The two women next to us quickly slid off their stools, left their coffees on the table, and marched out the door.

Thirteen

I had decided I would do my utmost to help Ashley in any possible way. "You're an escort?"

"Yeah, what'd you think I do, teach kids, or work in an office or something?"

"No, no, actually it makes sense, I guess. I mean, I didn't know Royal, Roy, was involved."

She nodded and took another sip. I noticed the lipstick on her coffee mug matched the color of her nails.

"He does your website?"

"Not exactly. No one actually has a website like you're thinking. Roy's got a number of sites, all over the world broken down by country. Like in the case of the US, the site lists the state and then the city. So for someone like me, well, I can go to Florida and Arizona in the winter or even London or Paris, if I want. Roy's service posts a visiting notice for me, and I get to work as much or as little as I want. It's pretty cool."

"And this works, I mean you get business, customers, clients?"

"Yeah, course it's all specialized. I mean they're vetted, you know, on his contact sites. Besides, we can list a complaint, and if the customer turns out to be some kind of jerk, they'll get blackballed, and then they can't use our services. Ever."

"Contact sites?"

"Yeah, before you can respond to my posting and set up an appointment, one of Roy's sites checks you out, makes sure your credit is good, you're not some lunatic or serial killer or God help me, a cop. They assign you an id number so you, as the customer, remain anonymous and all the transactions go through the site, no cash is exchanged, well, except for the tip," she said and raised her eyebrows. "Keeps us legal and safe."

I was curious. "What's your going rate?"

"Three-fifty an hour, goes up from there, depending," she said then looked at her watch. "Look, we should finish up, Tony's gonna be here any minute. Here's the deal, I'm down about fifteen percent over the last two months. This shit is hitting me right were it hurts, in my pocketbook. I told Roy, 'get it fixed baby or I gotta cut you loose.' You know?"

I nodded like I did know, although nothing could be further from the truth. "Let me do some brainstorming, Ashley. I'm thinking, just an old fashioned second pair of eyes might do the trick."

"Huh?" she said with a very blank look on her face.

"I plan to follow you around, see if we can't get whoever is taking all those pictures."

"Oh yeah, got it. Of course, I don't want you getting in the way. My clients are pretty high class and very private. It could be bad for business if they saw you lurking behind a palm tree in the hotel lobby or something. You know?"

A guy suddenly walked up behind Ashley, "Hey, baby, everything all right here?" he said, giving me the cold stare as he spoke.

"Hi, Tony, yeah, don't worry, he's okay. This is that investigator guy Roy called about. He's gonna find out who's been jacking me around."

"That so," Tony said, looking at me sideways, nodding with a half-smile on his face like he wasn't about to believe it.

"Hi, I'm Dev Haskell," I said and extended my hand. I didn't like the guy already, and he'd only been here for a couple of seconds.

He half snorted then said, "Haskell, I heard of you. You're the movie star."

"You're in movies?" Ashley half-shouted.

Heads turned. "No, no, it wasn't anything, believe me, and it was a long time ago."

"It was what you might call one of them cameo appearance deals, a reality video before reality shows. And now you're supposed to find out who's been doing this shit? Yeah, right," Tony said.

"I'm gonna try. It appears no one else has been able to do much. That's most likely why Mr. Baker contacted me. You wouldn't happen to have any ideas, would you, Tony?"

"I'm working on a couple of things. Yeah, I've got some ideas."

"Well, if you come up with anything, please be sure to share it with me. Look, Ashley, I'll be in touch, I want to get back to Royal and go over a couple of things. Is it all right if I give you a call tomorrow?"

"Let me call you. I've got your number. Grab my bags there will you, Tony?" she said and indicated the shopping bags scattered across the floor.

"All that shit, what'd you—?"

"Just pick them up, Tony, and let's go. God, you don't have to make a federal case out of it. I'm the one who had to go shopping for the last three hours, I'm beat, my feet are killing me, and I could use something just a little stronger than this latte right now."

"Okay, okay."

"Come on," she said, then slung that gigantic purse over her shoulder and marched off without saying goodbye. A number of heads turned as she strutted past, all the while continuing to read pain-in-the-ass Tony the riot act over her shoulder. I couldn't hear what she was saying, but I recognized the body language, and what a body.

There was something, make that a number of things I didn't like about Tony that had nothing to do with his movie star comment.

Fourteen

I left a message for Royal the following morning. Marilynn had let me know in no uncertain terms that she was the keeper of the gate, and I wasn't getting past. While waiting, I checked out Ashley's online presence. I visited five different sites, all listing escorts available in major cities around the world.

Ashley's profile name was exactly that, "Ashley," which led me to believe that wasn't her real name. She was willing to travel for a "to be determined" price and available in the twin cities for in-call at $350 per hour or out-call starting at $450. She was more expensive than any plumber I could think of, but then again. She would accept men, women, couples, two men, or two women with commensurate price increases.

You had to submit your credit card and list references to Royal's various sites, and then, upon approval, you would be able to contact her using a numerical ID and schedule an "appointment." Ashley was one of maybe twenty women listed in the Twin Cities area.

Royal's sites provided a secure vetting process as well as a variety of credit card, and PayPal billing options. I guess the business had moved a long way from just the simple "Buy me a drink?" line.

Ashley also had fifteen different images on her "photo album." The photos left nothing to the imagination as far as what, exactly, one would be paying for. All the images had the look of professionally-done studio shots, and for just a nanosecond, I wondered if the photographer had to pay the model.

There was a sixteenth image on Ashley's album, a bit out of focus, and obviously not part of the professional photoshoot. Ashley looked a tad bit disheveled while sitting in the passenger seat of a fairly trendy car. If I had to hazard a guess, I'd say it was her thug pal, Tony behind the wheel, but he was out of focus and partially cut off, so it was tough to tell.

Based on all the vehicles in the background, the photo looked to have been taken in a parking ramp of some sort. I made a mental note to ask both Ashley and Royal if the image had been posted recently. I was thinking it could have even been taken yesterday at The Mall.

I looked at sites for a half dozen other women, all equally beautiful, the women that is. None of them had anything like Ashley's amateur car image, which suggested she, specifically, was being targeted for some reason.

"Haskell Investigations," I said, tearing myself away from a half dozen images of a redheaded beauty in a bubble bath.

"Please hold for Mr. Baker," a no-nonsense voice replied.

"Happy to do that, Marilynn," I said, but she'd already put me on hold.

"Royal Baker."

"Hi, Royal, it's Dev Haskell. I met with Ashley yesterday."

"How did that go?"

"I suppose okay, amazingly she didn't want to come home with me." I waited a few moments but didn't get a response from Royal, so I pushed ahead. "Based on what she told me, I think some old fashioned monitoring with another pair of eyes might be in order. Let me ask you something. I just checked out her photos on your site, and—"

"Which site?"

"It's Compatibles," I said, looking at the address bar on my screen.

"Let me get it up here in a moment. There we go, and you're in her photo album?"

"Yeah, there's fifteen studio shots, then this one that—"

"Oh, damn it. God, how in the hell are they doing this? You're talking about this image where she's in the car and looks like she just pulled an all-nighter?"

"Yeah, I mean, it's not so bad. It's just obviously not in line with the other studio shots she has, very nice, by the way. I'm guessing it was taken on the fly, looks like a parking ramp of some sort."

"Yeah. Hell, it looks like she's working out of the back seat of a car."

"I met her out at The Mall of America yesterday afternoon. It could have been taken right after we met."

"Or before."

"To tell the truth, she was pretty well put together when we met. She looks like she's been through the mill in this shot. Any idea how long this has been up there, hours, days?"

"We're doing sweeps of her site twice a day, every day. So, this had to have been posted just in the past hour or so. Damn, that suggests whoever is doing this is aware of our schedule."

"So, you think they posted it sometime after ten?"

"Yeah, late morning to early afternoon are busy booking hours for evening appointments, we've been doing our sweeps just before that. Did you mention this to Ashley?"

"No, I'm waiting for her to call me."

"Dev, I'd appreciate it if you wouldn't say anything. I'd certainly make it worth your while. She can be somewhat temperamental, we're all at our wits end over this, and having Ashley fly off the handle again would only serve to satisfy whoever is behind this."

"No need to do anything, Royal. I won't mention it, but there's a good possibility she may have already seen it."

"Well, I haven't received one of her screaming phone calls, thankfully. I'm emailing someone as we speak. He'll have this removed within the next few minutes, barely eleven o'clock, so there's a pretty good chance she's still asleep."

I wanted to ask Royal about Ashley's butthead friend, Tony. I wanted to ask Royal about his business. I wanted to ask what his wife thought. In the end, I settled for, "Okay, Royal, I'm going to see about lining up some surveillance time around Ashley, I plan to coordinate with her, she said she'd call me, anything develops I'll let you know."

"Stay in touch," he said and hung up.

Fifteen

It had been a long day, and I knew if I headed over to The Spot it would only serve to make the day even longer, much longer. So I just went home. I was planning on making myself a decent dinner, meaning I would warm up some cold pizza and garlic bread. I was sure I'd left some in the fridge, but the garlic bread was nowhere to be found, and although the pizza delivery box was in the fridge, it was empty. I decided to watch a movie of no redeeming value and turn to the liquid diet, in my case, a glass of Maker's Mark bourbon on ice. Only there wasn't any. I could have sworn I had a fifth in the liquor cabinet. I ended up just eating candy bars.

My phone woke me the following morning. I was still on the couch, the candy bar bag was empty, and the sun was fairly high in the sky.

"Yeah," I answered, slowly coming awake.

"Dev?"

"That's me."

"Andy Lindbergh, did I catch you at a bad time?"

"No, Andy, sorry, just on another line, wrapping some business up."

"Want to call me back?"

"Nope, all taken care of. What can I do for you?"

"I've got a problem over here, wonder if you wouldn't mind stopping by."

"You want to tell me about it over the phone?"

"I've got some inventory items missing, special order stuff. I think if you could come over it might be easier to show you what I'm talking about. That will answer some questions and probably prompt some others."

I immediately thought Tommy Flaherty but didn't say anything. That idiot was probably doing a two-bit score on drugs of some sort, injecting embalming fluid or some stupid thing, blowing his chance at a good job, and putting himself back on the road to another conviction and more jail time. "You name the time, Andy."

"Well, the sooner, the better. Can you make it sometime today?"

"Let me cancel my meeting, and I'll be over there in an hour."

"You sure, Dev? I hate to be a pain."

"Not a problem, Andy. See you in an hour."

"Thanks, buddy, I appreciate it."

I put the coffee on, shaved, took a shower, got dressed, made some toast, gassed up my car, and picked up a couple of things at the grocery store on the way over to Andy's. I was ushered into his office as soon as Cathy, the receptionist, saw me walking into the lobby.

"Andy said I was to show you right in. He's waiting for you, Dev," she said, walking me rather quickly across the lobby and into Andy's office.

"Dev," Andy called as I stepped into his office. "Thanks for dropping everything and rushing over. Close the door on the way out, will you, Cathy. Grab a seat, Dev."

I waited until Cathy closed the door behind her, then asked, "What is it, Andy?"

"I wasn't sure at first, we had two go missing, and I was hoping it was just a shipping issue. Unfortunately, this last incident is local and a one of a kind design to boot. Not good for business."

"What are you missing?"

"Oh, sorry about that, I'm just so worked up over this. A coffin, three of them actually, as of this morning."

"Coffins? Someone's stealing coffins?"

"Yeah, afraid so, this last one was a special order, black walnut, hand carved with a family crest on the lid. It was supposed to be delivered yesterday. I heard from our client about five minutes before I called you. They've got the visitation scheduled for tomorrow. Christ on a bike, there's no way my vendor can turn around another in that short amount of time."

"Right off the top, a coffin doesn't strike me as something that can just walk out of here."

"True, but we ship quite a few on any given day."

"Define quite a few."

Andy clicked a couple of keys on his computer, waited a few seconds then said, "Yesterday we shipped twenty-three. The day before that, we shipped forty-seven. These go out anywhere from groups of five or ten to individual purchases loaded up in a hearse. We ship all over the country."

"And you're missing three."

"That I know of, I've got accounting going back over our shipping receipts for the past two months. We wouldn't have caught this latest one except that it was a special order, and we got that phone call from our customer, wondering when he was going to see his order."

"What are we talking dollar-wise here?"

"Start at fifteen hundred and head north. This latest one, special order, hand-carved with that family crest, black walnut, you're looking at about fifty-five-hundred."

"That's a lot of money to place in the ground."

"It's a very emotional decision for folks."

"Any ideas?"

"In all honesty, no, not really. But to tell the truth, I haven't had much time to think about it. Like I said until that phone call earlier this morning, I didn't have an inkling something like this was going on. Thus far, it looks like three units that we know of, in probably as many weeks."

I was thinking Tommy Flaherty, again. But what would he do with a coffin, let alone three? "Any chance it was just shipped to the wrong place, got mixed in with one of your larger orders?"

"Anything's possible, but that's a pretty slim option. We ID these in our system with unique, specific reference numbers, they're bar-coded, and they aren't showing up as having been shipped out anywhere."

"Andy, I'm still trying to get my head around this. What would someone do with these? I mean, is there a black market for coffins?"

"A black market? No, not that I'm aware of, doesn't mean one doesn't exist, but I'm not aware of it. Maybe someone would think it's funny, you know, a prank, use the thing for a dining room table or a guest bed, but not three of them."

I had a tough time seeing someone using a coffin as a guest bed.

"It's not like you could place one of these in the back of an SUV or something, they're too big even for most pickups. I've got my warehouse manager going over our security tapes, but the cameras really just monitor the exterior of the building, front, and back after hours. Security is activated when the last person leaves at night."

"When is that?" I asked and immediately thought of Tommy Flaherty again, working late until eight every night.

"I think most nights the cleaning crew is out of here by ten, maybe ten-thirty. They've been with us for a lot of years, Dev, it's a mother and two daughters. I would really be surprised if they were involved."

I sat and thought for a moment. "What about the possibility of an employee here on the inside, just loading someone up and they drive off."

"Possible, I suppose. I don't like to think like that."

"That's what I get paid to do, think like that. It's why I make the big bucks. Say someone with a hearse showed up, their inside contact loads them up, would something like that be possible?"

"We're running three separate bays just for hearses, that doesn't count the loading dock where the larger trucks pull in. I suppose it's possible, hell, at this point, anything is possible."

"And you don't have any security cameras on the inside?"

Andy shook his head.

"Those bays for the hearses, can you see from one to the other, or are they segmented, you know with walls between them?"

"Actually, there are walls between them."

"So, if a time was prearranged or someone asked for their favorite warehouse guy, conceivably, they might be able to pull this off."

"I suppose."

"I think for starters, I'd put in place a policy like nothing gets shipped out without two signature releases from your staff. The other thing, if you can identify these items, and you said that one was pretty specific, I'd maybe check out eBay."

"Oh God," Andy groaned.

"Yeah, just a thought. I remember a few years ago someone was stealing pacemakers from a hospital and attempted to sell the things on eBay. You mind if I go out there and just look around? You never know what might pop up."

"Please be my guest. Our warehouse manager is Milo. In fact, let me walk you back there and introduce you. As you might imagine, he's just a little testy about all this right now."

Sixteen

Milo Wasnik was in his mid-fifties and didn't look all that pleased to have me underfoot. Andy introduced me and then on his way out the door said, "Give Dev whatever he needs to get this figured out."

That left the two of us, Milo and me staring at one another. I was leaning against the door frame of Milo's small office. Milo was seated behind his desk, viewing what looked like a stack of security tapes. Meanwhile, three forklifts were busy loading boxes and barrels of product into a large semitrailer and a small truck. Four or five individuals were rolling carts or two-wheeled dollies in and out of the warehouse aisles loaded with more product.

I had the feeling Milo didn't get very many quiet moments even on a normal day, and today was turning out to be anything but normal.

"Andy says you got some bad news?" I said.

"That's the understatement. I've gone through a half-dozen security tapes, nothing but empty parking lots, and the occasional kids parked in the far corner for a petting session. I've got nine, make that ten more of these damn tapes to go through."

I explained my thoughts about some inside guy and a prearranged pick up.

"God, I suppose it's possible, but we have a pretty cohesive group. Everyone has been here for at least a couple of years. I hope that's not it."

"You aware of anyone on your staff experiencing money problems? Maybe a divorce, sick kid, mortgage headache?"

Milo shook his head. "We're all nothing if not dull. I'm not aware of anything like that, doesn't mean it might not be happening, but I'd usually hear about it."

"The people out there working, are they aware of this situation?"

"Yes and no. I had two guys running around trying to find that custom coffin for a good forty-five minutes this morning. That slowed us down while we looked for that damn thing. It's why they're all racing around out there right now. We're trying to get caught up. As you might imagine, something that size, it's not too easy to miss. I think we combed through the warehouse four separate times. It's definitely not here."

"So, just two other guys know?"

"For now, but like I said, it's a pretty tight-knit group. Give it another hour or two, and the word will be out."

"I'm not gonna bug your folks, but would you mind if I just looked around. Andy mentioned three bays for loading up vehicles, hearses. I'd like to look at them, maybe walk down a couple of aisles. Just get a feel for the place."

"Do you need me to go with you?" It was an offer, but Milo gave the polite, distinct impression he would prefer not to waste any more time with me.

"You know, thanks, but I'm just gonna stroll around, shouldn't be more than maybe fifteen minutes. I'll let you get back to looking at those security tapes. You come across anything let me know, here's my card," I said, handing him one of my cards.

Milo examined the card then leaned it up against a large white coffee mug with black lettering that read "Resurrection Cemetery," sitting on the corner of his desk. "Watch out for those forklifts. They're moving pretty fast."

He wasn't kidding. One of the forklifts zipped past me when I was no more than two steps out of his office. The driver gave me a deadpan nod, raced up a slight ramp, and into a large semitrailer. Once he passed, I hurried out of the way then headed for the three small loading bays.

They were located at the far end of the warehouse and were just as Andy described; private stalls that someone could back into and pick up a coffin. Two of the bays had a hearse parked in them with the back door open. The coffins were shrink-wrapped and brought into the loading bay on a four-wheeled cart. From there, they were rolled into the back of the hearse.

I watched as one of the warehouse guys scanned the barcode on the side of the coffin with a little handheld device. Then he adjusted the height of the cart to be level with the back door before he carefully pushed the coffin into the hearse. There were rollers embedded just inside the rear door of the hearse, and the guy made it look relatively effortless to roll the coffin inside. He closed the rear door on the hearse then handed the customer a receipt to sign. Once signed, he handed the guy a copy, waved good-bye, and headed for Milo's office. He gave me a nod as he passed and said, "How's it going," but didn't stop to wait for a reply.

It seemed a pretty standard shipping procedure. I watched the same process again in another bay. By the time I had finished watching, another hearse was backing into the bay. I'd check with Andy, but I guessed this was pretty much an all-day affair.

I wandered down a couple of aisles, everything from chemistry to holy cards was stacked on shelves going up probably ten feet high. In the far rear of the warehouse, the coffins were stacked on pallets and placed on shelves. A bald-headed driver was just lowering a coffin from about ten feet up with a forklift. He lowered the thing down to another guy with one of the four-wheeled carts, and together, they seemed to casually slide the coffin off the pallet and onto the cart. Then baldy drove off with the pallet still on the forks while the other guy wheeled the coffin back out to one of the bays.

"Dev? Hey, what are you doing out here?"

I turned and stared at Tommy Flaherty. He was dressed in casual slacks and a white golf shirt sporting a logo from the Copper Mountain Golf Course, Copper Mountain Colorado. Amazingly, I had a shirt just like that. I wondered what were the odds?

"Tommy, how's everything going? I keep hearing good things from Andy, man."

"Yeah, going pretty well. Course you know collections, it's never done, there's always at least one more account you'd like to help get back on track. What are you doing back here?"

"Oh, Andy wanted me to check some stuff."

"Check some stuff?"

I wasn't sure if I might have detected a hint of concern.

"Nothing major. I do some security system consulting. Andy was thinking of putting some cameras back here, but to tell you the truth, the area is so large, by the time it was wired and all setup, I don't think it would be worth the trouble."

"Is he missing inventory?"

"I don't think so, God, who'd want to steal holy cards and crucifixes?"

"Yeah, there is that. Hey, I better get these things pulled, someone is waiting for them up at the receptionist's desk," he said and waved what looked like an invoice as confirmation.

"They got you working in the warehouse now?"

"No, just the occasional person that comes in the front door. I just like to help out, you know, make myself useful wherever I can."

"Good for you, Tommy. I better head out, too. Nice to see you again." I didn't mention the golf shirt.

Seventeen

My phone rang just as I was pulling into my driveway that evening.

"Let me speak to Dev?"

I almost melted when I heard the sexy tone of Ashley's voice. I immediately envisioned a particular photo image of her, the one where the silk sheet was barely draped across her thighs, and she sat in the middle of a queen-size bed sucking on her index finger and looking hopeful. I imagined her whispering in my ear, which, since she was on the phone, was kind of what she was kind of doing.

"Hello, hello, can you hear me?"

"Oh, hi, Ashley, Just getting off a conference call here."

"Whatever. Hey, look, I've got an appointment tonight. At the Gresham. Tony always brings me then waits, but I was thinking if you wanted to do some of your surveillance and stuff, you could maybe check things out and see if you can catch the guy who's been doing this."

"What time will you be at the Gresham?"

"My appointment is at eight, just for an hour."

"Is that pretty standard?"

"The Gresham?"

"No, an hour appointment."

"Yeah, at least to start, but a lot of the time, they decide to go into extra innings if you know what I mean."

"Yeah, I'm following. I'll be there. Do you go in the main door?"

"Yeah, how else would I get in there?"

"There's a second-floor entrance from the parking ramp."

"Oh, no, I'll go in the front door."

"There's a circular drive up to the front door. Have Tony drop you off right at the door. I'll be in front checking things out then follow you inside. If you see me, don't acknowledge me."

"You sure this is gonna work. To tell you the truth, it sounds more than a little sketchy."

"No, I'm not sure it's gonna work, but it's a start. Let's see what happens from there."

"And Royal is paying you, right? You're not thinking of charging me are you?"

"Royal will be paying me."

"Okay, then that's fine," she said and hung up.

I climbed the steps to my porch, unlocked the front door, and made a beeline for my closet. There was an empty hanger where my Copper Mountain golf shirt usually hung. As a matter of fact, there were maybe a half dozen empty hangers. I couldn't recall if they suggested missing shirts or nothing more than extra hangers, but I couldn't worry about that right now.

I was at the Gresham a half-hour early. The circular drive was made of red brick pavers and wrapped around a very nice garden filled with flowers and precisely pruned bushes. The entire area was boarded by a three-foot trimmed hedge of green, leafy plants with little black berries. A broad sidewalk ran right up the middle of the garden, and in the exact center of the garden, two wooden park benches sat opposite one another.

I sat on one of the benches, a couple, apparently overserved, sat on the other bench, discussing if they should get a room. From what I could pick up, they'd been attending a wedding in one of the ballrooms, and now their intentions had progressed to the consummation part of the evening. I'd taken their photo for them with her cellphone maybe five minutes earlier.

I held a newspaper attempting to look like I might be reading, but I was scanning the area nonstop. Thus far, I had discovered absolutely nothing. I probably checked my watch every minute for twenty-five minutes, from about ten minutes before eight until eight-fifteen when Ashley finally arrived.

Idiot Tony was driving her in that sporty blue thing that had been in the blurry image posted online the other day. He stopped across the street from the hotel, and I watched while they seemed to argue in the car. I couldn't make out what was being said, but I could hear the tone from where I sat. More than one couple walking past gave a brief glance toward Tony's car then picked up their pace.

After a few minutes of dramatics, Ashley got out of the car, stuck her tongue out at Tony then slammed the car door. Tony sped off down the street causing one car to slam on the brakes, and lean on his horn. So much for a subtle entry.

Ashley pranced up the sidewalk in an exaggerated manner, placing one foot directly in front of the other like some fashion model strutting down the runway. Once again, all heads were turned, including the guy seated across from me, at least until his date hit his arm and whined, "Gary."

Ashley paused in front of me, looked down, and said, "Get anyone, yet?" which pretty much ended my efforts out in front of the hotel.

"No, not yet. Why don't you go keep your appointment, and I'll follow you in, you're already twenty minutes late."

"It's magic," she scoffed. "Works like a charm every time, they're so revved up by the time I knock on the door, they're usually only good for about five minutes. Sometimes I don't even have to get undressed."

Charming, I thought, then folded my newspaper and followed a discrete distance behind her.

The mood seemed to have changed decidedly with the couple seated across from me. He appeared to be pleading, and she had her arms crossed and continued to shake her head from side to side. A reaction to Ashley's personal brand of magic, unfortunately, I was very familiar with the body language.

We entered the hotel, past a fawning valet and concierge, both of whom greeted Ashley with a "Good evening, enjoy your time at the Gresham, madam." It made me wonder if perhaps they knew her on sight or at least were familiar with her particular line of work.

She waited for me to catch up with her at the bank of elevators then said, "I can take it from here. I'll be down in about a half-hour."

"I thought you had an hour appointment?"

"Like I said, it's magic." The elevator door opened and she stepped in then looked past me, seemingly emotionless as the doors closed and the elevator rose up to the sixth floor.

Eighteen

Tony stepped in through the revolving front door a moment later and made a beeline for the bar. I waited a couple of minutes looking for I don't know what in the lobby then followed. On my way to the bar, I glanced out the front door to the benches in the garden. The guy was still sitting there, talking to someone on his cellphone, and his date was nowhere to be seen.

Tony was seated at the far end of the bar, staring into a pint of beer. Not surprisingly, no one was seated around him. I figured anyone with any sense had gotten up and left the moment he'd arrived.

"Mind if I join you, Tony?"

"Not like I can stop you."

I didn't feel like it, but I pulled out a stool anyway.

"So, how's it feel being a big movie star?"

"That's pretty old news, Tony, where'd you ever hear about that."

"I got my sources."

"Sure you do."

"You see anything, catch some guy taking pictures?" He asked in a tone suggesting there wasn't a chance in hell I would have.

"Nope, sorry to disappoint, Tony, but so far, the only guy I've seen taking pictures tonight was me, right out there in that front garden."

He smirked and then shook his head like he couldn't believe how stupid I was. I've maybe done the same thing before too, and to tell the truth, I was thinking about doing it now after dealing with him and Ashley.

"Hey, I thought you were going to pull into the circular drive tonight and drop Ashley off right at the front door."

"Yeah, she was bitching about that, but what a pain in the ass. I didn't feel like doing it."

"Here's the thing, Tony. If you did that, and there was someone outside waiting to take her picture, that might have forced them to run and catch up or at least have done something that might have caught our attention, and we may have been able to figure out who's behind this. Since you decided not to do that, we really didn't have much of a chance."

"So you're saying it's my fault you can't nail the guy, that it? All of a sudden, it's my fault?"

"No. What I'm saying is, if you keep on doing the same thing time after time, you're probably going to get the same result. If we have a plan, maybe we could all agree to work together and see if we can't nail the individual who has been photographing Ashley."

"Yeah, right, so all of a sudden, it's my fault. Screw you," he said, then took a long sip of beer and stared at me over the rim of his glass.

The bartender stepped over to us at this point, laid a circular mat for a glass down in front of me, and said, "What can I get you, sir."

"Nothing for me, I was just leaving."

Tony snickered and took another long sip.

The jukebox was playing some nineties number I recognized, but I couldn't come up with the name. I glanced around the barroom. It was barely half full. Still, I figured there were too many witnesses and so I left.

Nineteen

I waited in the lobby with an eye on the elevators. I was sitting in a comfortable leather chair reading my newspaper when I wasn't watching people walk past toward the elevators. The foot traffic seemed to have a definite flow. People coming into the hotel were either picking up their key at the front desk, then heading toward the elevators, or coming into the hotel and heading directly toward the elevators. Not a lot of folks seemed to be leaving the building.

I was seated in one of three groupings of brown leather couches and chairs. The lobby was wide and very long with white marble floor tiles covered by large, thick oriental rugs and period floor lamps. The walls were paneled in dark oak to a height of about five feet, then painted gold color with stencil designs running just above the paneling and just below the elegant plaster molding bordering the fourteen-foot ceiling.

At the far end of the lobby, closest to the bank of elevators, a large marble fireplace had a nice fire blazing. Maybe a half dozen people were gathered around it, drinking glasses of wine, laughing, and chatting.

Ashley exited the elevator some hours later. By now, the lobby was quiet. The crowd by the fireplace had dwindled down to just two people. I watched Ashley as she made her way to the barroom, oblivious to me almost asleep in a chair. I scanned the lobby, but couldn't see anyone paying any attention, well, except for the guy by the fireplace, but he only gave her a passing glance. She didn't appear quite as well put together as she had when she arrived. I glanced at my watch before I followed her into the barroom. It was after midnight.

She hadn't been more than a minute ahead of me and was already locked in an argument with Tony when I entered the bar.

"Look at you, God, you're high again, all screwed up," he said. Then took a sip, he'd apparently switched from beer to bourbon or Scotch somewhere during the past three and a half hours.

"You don't know," she said, then ran a hand through her hair and steadied herself by grabbing hold of the back of a bar stool.

"Ash, you still got some blow on your lip, please don't tell me that's how you got paid, again, Jesus."

"Well, you're drunk."

"That's because your thirty-minute little love-fest with the boss man went on for about four hours," Tony said, then focused on me just coming into view behind Ashley. "What the hell do you want? I thought you left."

Ashley turned and attempted to focus on me, her pupils looked dilated and idiot Tony was right, she did have powder under her nose. She seemed to weave back and forth in place for a moment then said, "Did you get the bastard?"

"He didn't get shit. Didn't get the guy. Didn't see the guy. Nothing, just like I told you."

She spun around, and half-shouted, "Shut the hell up, Tony." Then she turned back toward me. "Tell me you got him."

"Nope. Didn't see a thing. Doesn't mean he wasn't here. Maybe he still is for all we know."

Tony glanced around the room. There were only four other people in the place, a table of three involved in an animated conversation and a guy sitting off by himself in a distant corner focused on some college football game on the flatscreen.

"You gotta be kidding. You didn't see him, nothing?"

"Not that I could determine."

"What in God's name have you been doing all night? What the hell am I paying you for?" Ashley snapped.

"Yeah, what are we…?"

"You're not paying me, either one of you," I said, looking directly at Tony. "You didn't do what I told you to do. Simple as it was, you didn't follow the plan. You arrived almost a half-hour late, Ashley. And Tony, you didn't drop Ashley off where we planned, and now you're wondering why I couldn't spot some individual who probably got fed up about the same time I did, only he could leave. Unfortunately, I'm stuck here talking to the two of you."

Tony started to move off his bar stool, but his foot was wrapped around the leg, and he did a slow motion-tumble into Ashley. She fell backward, shrieking, and they both went down on the floor.

"You bastard, you did that on purpose," Tony yelled at me from down on the floor.

The three people at the table had stopped their animated conversation and stared at us. The bartender remained at the far end of the bar. Ashley had rolled over and was up on all fours, but couldn't seem to move past that point. What you could see of her black thong was directed at Tony's face. The lone guy watching the college football game sighed as he stood up and slowly made his way over to us. He helped Ashley up off the floor then glanced down at Tony. "Can you get up?"

"What's your problem, asshole?" Tony asked from the floor, looking like he might have some trouble focusing from that distance.

"Hotel security, I think it might be best if everyone headed up to their rooms. Let's keep it a nice quiet night, okay folks?"

"This bastard here—"

"Sir," he said to Tony. "This probably isn't the best time or the best place. Maybe sleep on it, and we could discuss this in the morning."

Tony gave him a look.

"Or, we could call the police, and you could sort it out down at the station. I would prefer not to do that, but I will."

"Come on, Ashley, get your ass out of here," Tony said, standing up. He set his face with a determined look then staggered out of the bar. When he reached the door, he turned around and yelled, "You're fired, Haskell. You hear me, you are so fired, man."

"I'll say, ditto that," Ashley said, then strutted out the door after Tony.

"Whoa, you work for those two," the security guy asked.

"No, thank God."

"Maybe wait a minute or two, and then you should probably leave too, sir. Have a pleasant evening." He smiled, then turned and followed Ashley and Tony out of the barroom.

Twenty

That's what they said, "You're fired," Louie asked. He was wearing a wrinkled, blue pinstripe suit, and he'd already managed to dribble coffee down the front of an otherwise clean, starched shirt. It wasn't quite ten in the morning.

"Yeah, and get this, I'm not even working for them. Royal Baker hired me to check them out, see if I could find out who the hell has been taking her picture and posting it online."

"And you never saw anyone?"

I'd been attempting to peer in the third-floor apartment windows across the street, but thus far, I hadn't had any luck. I put the binoculars down and spun around in my office chair to face Louie.

"Not only did I not see anyone, now *I* want to take a picture of her looking shitty and post it online, or at least get a dartboard-sized copy. Not a nice lady and man, does she ever deserve that jackass guy she's with."

"They both sound like a real piece of work. You think she makes money doing that stuff?"

"Who knows? I mean, yeah, she could theoretically be making some dough, but if she usually works the way she was operating last night, she probably ended up paying whoever her customer was, or took the payment in nose candy."

"Charming."

I placed a call to Royal, actually, I phoned and spoke with Marilynn, who said, "Mr. Baker is unavailable just now. Who may I ask is calling?"

"It's Dev Haskell, Marilynn."

"Oh," she said, sounding more than a little disappointed.

"Can I leave a message to have him call me when he has a free moment?"

"Yes, I'll see that he gets the message. Will there be anything else?"

"No, thank you."

My phone rang before I could refocus the binoculars.

"Please hold for Mr. Baker."

"Hello," Royal said a moment later.

"Hi, Royal, Dev Haskell."

"Yeah, any new developments, Dev? Did you get our man?"

"Yes and no. I didn't see anyone, and Tony and Ashley informed me that I was fired last night."

"What?"

I went on to explain the previous night's events, how the two of them were possibly incapable of following the simplest of plans. I mentioned Tony's confrontational nature and Ashley's rather unprofessional attitude, although I wasn't quite sure, given her line of work, that unprofessional was the word.

"I'm sorry to hear all this, Dev. And you didn't see anyone fitting the bill. No guy following her, maybe lurking in the bushes or the lobby?"

"No, sorry, nothing like that, Royal. But, to tell the truth, they both seemed oblivious to any sense of security. And Ashley's entry from the time she stepped out of the car until the elevator doors closed and brought her up to I think it was the sixth floor, we're only talking a minute, maybe a minute-and-half. With any luck, your guy wasn't around. Who knows? Maybe your security sweeps have finally done the trick."

"We'll see, for the time being, let me smooth things over with the two of them. Tony can be difficult, but he's got Ashley's best interests at heart. And Ashley is nothing if not headstrong, but the poor thing has been under a lot of stress lately with all of this."

"Well, keep me posted. In the meantime, if you could email me your list of disgruntled former employees, I'll be doing some research in that area."

"It sounds as though that may just be our best bet, at least at this point. I'll have Marilynn email the list to you this morning. Let's stay in touch," Royal said and hung up. It wasn't ten minutes later when the list arrived in my email.

Twenty-one

Royal's list of disgruntled employees was less than I had hoped for, a lot less. There were just three names on the thing. One guy was located in India, another in the Philippines, and the third was in Denver. Maybe I was missing something, but at least on the surface, they didn't seem to be very likely suspects to be following an escort around St. Paul and taking photographs.

The list had contact information, including phone numbers. I attempted to phone the guy in India first. It took me three tries, but I finally got through, or at least it was ringing.

"Hello?"

"Hello, I'm calling from the United States, I'd like to speak with Chetan, please."

"What is this in regard to?" he asked. His accent was heavy, and I had to focus to understand what he was saying.

"Is this Chetan?"

"Indeed, it is."

That seemed good enough for me. If the guy was at home in India he wasn't taking pictures of someone in

St. Paul. "Thank you," I said and hung up. I had the same result with my call to the Philippines, although the guy I called, Nick Santos, sounded a lot crabbier. Then again, I'd called at a quarter to one in the morning, his time, so I had probably gotten him out of a sound sleep.

The Denver call went to a guy named Mickey Cray. After the crabby response I'd gotten from the Philippines, I checked the time difference first, just an hour behind. I dialed, and a recording came on the line, "This call may be recorded." Then the phone rang, and a woman answered on the third ring.

"Hello," she sounded nice, even with just the one word.

"Hi, I'm calling for Mickey Cray."

"Speaking," she replied.

That caught me off guard. "Oh, Ms. Cray, I'm sorry to bother you. I received your name from a friend of mine, actually. Do you work with computers, website design things along that line?"

"I'm a programmer if that's what you mean. I'm sorry, I don't believe I caught your name."

"My name is Haskell, Dev Haskell. I received your name from a friend of mine and—"

"A friend? You're calling from a six-five-one area code, isn't that Minnesota?" she asked as the sweetness vanished from her voice.

"Why, yes, it is, I hope I haven't called too early, I—"

"Who gave you my name?"

"Mr. Baker," I said wishing, I could take those last two words back even before she exploded, and I felt the heat coming through the phone.

"Baker, you mean that bastard, Royal Baker? What? My restraining order and the lawsuit didn't get his attention. So, now he's got you doing his dirty work. Let me tell you something, Mr. Hackle, I'm reporting you to my attorney, and he'll be in touch with your local police. I've captured your number on my cell, and for your information, all my calls are recorded. You can join your good friend, Mr. Baker in the lawsuit. How does that sound?"

"Nice talking to you," I said and hung up.

"What the hell was that?" Louie asked, looking up from a file. "I could hear her screaming all the way over here."

"Apparently not a real big fan of Royal Baker."

"Why were you calling her?"

"Baker emailed me a list of disgruntled former employees."

"I'd say that pretty much fits the description of that last woman."

"Yeah, anyway, they're all out of town, two of the three are out of the US. I figured if I called them, and they answered, then they couldn't be the guy taking the photos of Ashley and posting them. That last witch was in Denver."

"Tell me you're kidding."

"Kidding? No, why?"

"Dev, didn't that last woman just scream at you that she's got your number on her cell?"

"Yeah."

"So, even though she lives in Denver, she could have been out in front of the building here, and she would be able to answer her *cellphone*. All your call did, other than piss her off was maybe confirm her phone number, but not where she's located right now."

It suddenly seemed so obvious. I did a half glance out the window just to see if there was some woman looking really mad pacing out on the street. Fortunately, my phone rang before Louie had a chance to point out any further flaws in my logic.

"Haskell Investigations."

"Dev, Andy."

"Hi, Andy, how are things?"

"Well, if you mean are we missing anything else, the answer is a qualified 'no,' at least nothing we're aware of at this point."

"I'll take that as good news. What can I do for you?"

"Milo drew a blank on reviewing those security tapes. The good news is there seemed to be no activity. Then again, the bad news is just that, there seemed to be no activity. What did you come up with wandering around?"

"Nothing, really, other than you're a lot busier back there than I ever imagined." My phone beeped, signaling another call coming in. "Can I call you back, Andy. I've got a call coming in I have to take, probably be back to you in about five minutes."

"Later," Andy said and hung up.

"Haskell Investigations."

"Hold for a call from Mr. Baker," Marilynn said, and then the phone rang, Royal picked up halfway through the first ring.

"Dev?"

"Hi, Royal, what's up?"

"What's up is the two images I just had Marilynn email to you. They've been purged from our sites, but they were definitely taken last night. It's the same outfit Ashley was wearing, and she's not the kind of woman to wear the same outfit twice."

I wondered how Royal knew what Ashley had on last night, but didn't go there. "I'm going to my email right now, give me a few seconds here, Royal. Say while we're waiting, can you give me any info on the disgruntled list? Anything I should know about?"

"You mean is one of them our stalker. Honestly, any of them could be. I've never met Santos, the guy from the Philippines, although from all reports he's brilliant. Chetan, the Indian, the same. Both geniuses, but greedy and it would be just like them to attack someone like Ashley in an effort to get back at me."

"If they're the geniuses you say they are, wouldn't it be more true to form for them to plant a virus or something on your site. Something that might cripple your entire operation, shut the thing down. It would seem to me that would be a bigger danger than just posting photos of Ashley, pain in the ass that it is."

"Well, just wait until you see these latest two."

I noticed Royal didn't mention Mickey Cray, and I didn't say anything. "I'm just downloading your images now. Give me a minute. Here's the first one coming up."

The image that spread across my screen was Ashley, all right. She was sticking her tongue out, presumably at Tony, although you really couldn't see him. It was just before she'd slammed the car door and walked up to me on her way into the Gresham. So much for following my plan and getting dropped off at the front door.

I clicked on the second image, and it filled my screen. It was Tony, well a view from the back of Tony. Ashley's legs were wrapped around him, and her head was over his shoulder and looking skyward. The two of them appeared to be engaged in a sexual act on the hood of Tony's snarky blue car.

"Interesting. Well, there you go, Royal. I think I mentioned in the not too distant past that the two of them seemed to be oblivious to security. I guess a picture's worth a thousand words, in this case, two pictures. The shot with Ashley sticking her tongue out, that was when Tony couldn't be bothered to drop her off at the front door of the Gresham like we had agreed. The other shot, this one on the hood of the car, what are the odds someone might show up to claim one of those cars parked around them. Of course, what does that matter when you've got some guy with a camera right there to record it for history and send it around the world so everyone can see it?"

"I think we should probably all sit down and talk," Royal said.

"I'm willing to do that, but in all honesty, until they start paying attention to what's going on around them, I'm not sure it's going to make much of a difference."

"Could it hurt?" Royal asked.

Twenty-two

I decided to swing past my place on the way over to Royal's office. I wasn't looking forward to sitting down with Tony and Ashley. In fact, I was ready to tell Royal I quit, and he could figure out another way of catching whoever was posting the pictures instead of wasting my time. On my way home, I put a call into Heidi just to give her a heads up that things weren't going the best with Royal's client, I ended up leaving a message.

I pulled into the open spot directly in front of my house. I stepped inside my front door and felt something wasn't right, but I couldn't quite put my finger on it. Everything seemed to be okay. I strolled through the first floor and out into my kitchen. Did I smell pizza? Maybe it was just the restaurant across the street getting ready for their noon business. The sink was wet, but there didn't seem to be a dripping faucet. I cautiously walked upstairs with my ears perked for the slightest sound. My closet light was turned on, but maybe I'd left it that way. I certainly couldn't recall. I thought again about the Copper Mountain golf shirt that Tommy Flaherty was wearing yesterday at Andy's. With all the Ashley nonsense going on, I'd forgotten about it for the moment.

My phone rang at that point, "Haskell Investigations."

"Hi, Dev, returning your call," Heidi said.

"Oh yeah, thanks for calling back," I said then made my way back to the first floor. "Look, Heidi, I'm on my way to meet with Royal Baker and that client of his who was having the online harassment problems. I think I'm going to tell him I'm not the guy for the job, and well, I just wanted to give you heads up. I don't think this will screw up anything you might be working on, but just wanted to be sure."

"All I'm working on is trying to show him a number of options. I haven't gotten any further on that front than the last time we talked. What's the problem is it too techy for you?"

"No, the problem is his client is a major pain in the ass. Well, she and her jackass boyfriend or whatever the guy is. To tell you the truth, I just don't have the patience to put up with the attitude."

"Gee, there's a surprise, because you're such a patient, understanding guy otherwise."

"I knew you'd see it my way."

"Believe me, I was just kidding, Dev, the last thing you are, is patient. Thanks for checking, but do whatever you want to do, I don't have a problem with it."

"Great, hey, you doing anything tonight, free for dinner?"

"I could be, what did you have in mind?"

I wanted to say a chilled bottle of wine and Heidi's bed but settled for, "Nothing in particular. You pick the place, and I'll drive, or I can bring something over, whatever you feel like."

"I've got an end of day conference call, and I would love to just kick back tonight. Would you settle for a late-night dinner in my kitchen, say maybe eight, I'll even pick it up if you want."

Perfect. "Okay, you pick up dinner, but let me bring the wine. Prosecco to your liking?"

"Oh, God. I'd love it."

Me too, I thought, the perfect end to a pain in the butt day. "I'll see you around eight."

Twenty-three

Marilynn descended in the private elevator then brought me up to Royal's office. She seemed deep in thought, and other than a brisk "Hello," she didn't utter a word. Ashley had apparently been with Royal for a while, and when he did answer the phone, Marilynn then had to knock on his office door. He opened the door after a long moment. "Yes, Dev, come in, come in, thanks for making the time, Ashley is already here," he said then stood off to the side so I could enter.

Ashley was half stretched out on the couch in a rather unlady-like pose and ignored me as I entered. I detected a trace of powder beneath her nose as she wiggled her shoulders back and forth then tugged her blouse down from either side of her waist in an effort to straighten it out and pull herself together. I noticed a couple of the small cushions from the couch had been knocked to the floor. Royal picked them up and casually tossed them back on the couch.

"Hi, Ashley, how's it going?" I asked, hoping to start things off on a more positive note.

"Are you kidding me? Didn't you see my site? You completely missed him. He had all the time in the world to take those pictures, but since you had your head up your ass, you let him get away."

"I don't know how much time he had, I'm sure he liked watching the two of you on the hood of Tony's car, but that was after you fired me. And as for the shot of you sticking your tongue out, I suppose if you hadn't sat there arguing with Tony, if you'd done like I asked, gotten out of the car at the front door, it could have been avoided. But, what the hell would I know? You obviously know better, things certainly seem to be working in your favor."

"Royal, do something here," she said.

"Dev, please have a seat. Let's see if we can't work together here and come up with a plan."

"I just want this bastard caught and then castrated," Ashley said, then crossed her arms, put on a disgusted look, and stared at the floor.

"Royal, any luck with your tech folks finding out how this guy is gaining access?"

Royal shook his head. "Thus far, we're unable to find any trace of an unwarranted intrusion."

"Meaning?"

"Meaning, it has to be coming from within our system. What did you find out with our list of disgruntled employees?"

"I'm pretty sure you can eliminate them."

"Oh, that's just great. See, I told you he was absolutely worthless," Ashley said, then rolled her eyes.

Royal looked surprised and signaled a calming motion with his hand, then said, "What makes you so sure, Dev?"

"Well, for starters none, of them were in town last night."

"How do *you* know that?" Ashley said, making it sound more like an accusation than a question.

"I talked to them," I said and smiled sweetly. "Santos was in the Philippines, asleep. Your friend Chetan was in India, getting ready for bed. And the always charming Ms. Cray was in Denver and threatened me with a lawsuit. No way any of them could have been here last night and taken those photos then made it back to Denver, let alone to the far side of the globe."

"You don't know that," Ashley snapped.

"Well, just for starters, what time were you screwing on the hood of Tony's car? It had to be close to one in the morning. Even if Ms. Cray grabbed a red-eye out of here this morning, she wouldn't be able to make it back to Denver and then post those images before I called. And even if she did." I turned to face Royal. "I think you just stated your guys couldn't detect any outside intrusion."

"Actually, I think the term I used was unwarranted."

"Okay, unwarranted, but it's still the same. Say one of these folks had someone local taking those photos, then what? Send them to their computer or iPhone so they could somehow get past your security, undetected? I suppose it's possible, but it's a pretty slim chance."

"So, what's your great idea?" Ashley said.

"Well, for starters, I think you should probably confine your lovemaking to your own home or place of business, maybe take a pass on using the hood of a car in a parking ramp, at least for the time being."

"Ahem," Royal cleared his throat to get things back on track. "Do you have a suggestion, Dev?"

"Along with being able to post these images, whoever is involved obviously has access to Ashley's appointment calendar. I have two suggestions. The first would be for you to establish some other method for Ashley to get appointments. It could be as simple as a phone call confirming."

"That's gonna screw me royally. I might as well go back to just stripping for tips."

"The second thing I would recommend is setting up a fake appointment, using your normal procedure, and see if we can't set a trap and capture this person."

"I like that," Royal said and looked to Ashley for approval.

Ashley gave a bored shrug and said, "Whatever. I just want this all to stop. It's hitting me right in the damn pocketbook."

Royal gave an understanding nod, then flashed a smile in my direction and stood as he said, "Give us a little time here, Dev, and we'll be in touch." He walked over to the door and opened it, then summoned Marilynn to escort me down to the lobby.

Once he closed the door, I heard him ask Ashley, "Are you all right?" but couldn't hear anything beyond that.

Twenty-four

I had some time, and apparently, my headache wasn't bad enough, so I swung past Andy's to see if he had anymore information.

"No, I guess the good news is everything seems to be back to normal, at least for the past forty-eight hours. Took your advice, Milo is getting everything double checked as it's going out the door. I'm still at a loss. It's not like you can slip one of those coffins in your pocket and just walk out of here. And, I really don't want to contemplate one of our staff being involved, we've got a great team back there. They've all been with us for quite a while."

"You aware of any out of the workplace difficulty someone might be having, divorce, mortgage, a sick child or spouse, and there's medical bills, something like that, maybe college tuition?"

"No, nothing that I'm aware of, you might want to check with Milo, but I haven't heard of anything."

"I already asked him. He wasn't aware of anything either. What about access to the warehouse? Can anyone just walk back there?"

"You mean anyone in the company, yeah, sure. Just for starters, the bathrooms and the break room are back there. But, if you're suggesting could anyone just wander around out there, not really. You got a taste of how busy it is back there the other day, and it's like that every day. Not only would someone stick out who didn't belong, but frankly, they'd be in the way."

I didn't want to mention it, but I had to. "I ran into Tommy Flaherty when I was wandering around back there."

"Really," Andy said, then shot me a puzzled look.

"Yeah, he said a customer was in the lobby and had placed an order, and he was pulling some items. He had an invoice in his hand."

"Oh yeah, of course, that makes sense. Cathy has to stay chained to the receptionist desk, and Tommy would be the logical choice to fill the order, especially something that's just a few items. Anything larger and Cathy might generate an invoice, but then she'd send the person around to the loading dock for pickup. Do you think there's a problem?"

"With Tommy? No, I'm just trying to cover all the bases. You haven't been out there unattended, have you?"

"Me wandering out there unattended would create a problem," Andy said and smiled.

"Mind if I pop my head into Milo's office? I just want to thank him for his time yesterday and touch base."

"Be my guest."

"I'll just be a minute or two. Then I'll head out. I want to check some online areas."

"Online?" Andy said as I was getting up.

"You know eBay, a couple of places like that. Maybe someone's stupid enough to put a unique item like that carved coffin up for sale."

Andy nodded, then said, "Keep me posted."

The warehouse area was just as busy as the last time I was back there. I stuck my head into the office. "Milo."

He looked up from some a printout and a cloud seemed to pass over his face the moment he recognized me.

"Just wanted to say thanks for your time yesterday. Andy said you drew a blank on those security tapes."

"About six wasted hours of time I didn't have," he said.

"Thanks all the same for going over them."

He seemed to relax a bit then asked, "You learn anything?"

"Yeah, look out for forklifts."

That earned a momentary smile.

"Still working it, we'll see what develops. You learn anything, or something doesn't look right, let Andy know," I said.

"That's what I planned on doing," he said.

"Thanks again, Milo I'm out of your hair."

Twenty-five

On the way home from Andy's, I stopped and picked up some Prosecco from Solo Vino. I put the three bottles in the fridge to chill and decided it might be a good idea to do some laundry so I could show up at Heidi's with a clean shirt.

I was stuffing the laundry into the washer, filling it once again to overcapacity when I pulled out a shirt from the bottom of my laundry basket. It was a white golf shirt with a logo that read Copper Mountain Golf Course, Copper Mountain, Colorado. The last time I'd done laundry was two weeks ago, and even I could remember that far back. I hadn't worn this shirt, but I knew who had. The question was, how did Tommy Flaherty get it in the first place? And then, how did he get the shirt into my laundry?

I remembered thinking I smelled food earlier, just before I drove over to Royal's Office. Was Tommy able to get in my house anytime he wanted? I turned the washer on, then went around and checked all the basement windows. They were locked and probably hadn't been opened in years. The first-floor windows were all secure. In my mind, that left only one option, unfortunately, Tommy had a set of keys.

The couple of nights he stayed with me, he could have taken my keys and had copies made. I lived close enough to the hardware store, it wouldn't have taken more than fifteen minutes.

I started thinking back to the missing food, the sport coat I thought I'd left at some woman's house. The shirts I couldn't find and then just by chance the golf shirt I saw him wearing yesterday.

The moment Heidi answered her door, I forgot about Tommy Flaherty. She was wearing very tight white shorts, a silky white top, apparently no bra, and white sandals with little colored flowers on the strap. I gave the sandals a peripheral glance and returned to the blouse.

"We're eating Thai, with Dim Sum," she said.

"That'll be a nice change," I said.

She looked at me strangely as she closed the door behind us, "I think it's what we had the last time, in fact, you brought it. Remember?"

"I was kidding. Here, let me put these in your fridge, Prosecco. How did your conference call go?" I asked and headed for her kitchen.

"Oh, thanks. The call? About what I expected, no surprises, just some hand-holding. The way the market is right now everyone has the jitters, the best thing to do is stay put. They just need to hear that, and they did.

They'll be fine until the next media-induced panic attack."

"Maybe you should free up one of those hedge funds, and the two of us could fly out to Vegas, double the money over the weekend and make everyone happy."

"Occasionally, some fool tries that, and guess what? It never ever works. So, how'd things go with Royal?" she asked, then seemed to spend an inordinate amount of time bending over and placing two of the prosecco bottles in her almost empty fridge. Her very small black thong was visible through the white shorts. I just stood there and took in the view.

"Did you hear me?" she said, standing up. "How did things go with Royal?"

"Well, I didn't quit if that's what you're asking. How'd they go? I guess okay. He's going to alter some procedure with his client having all the problems, and we'll see where it goes from there. How well do you know him?" I said, then pushed a glass of Prosecco across the counter toward her as she sat down on a kitchen stool. There were a half dozen white takeout food containers with wire handles sitting on the end of the counter surrounded by about three dozen little plastic envelopes of soy sauce.

"How well do I know him? Not very, I mean I've studied his company, they're very profitable. They do programming, websites, IT things," Heidi said.

"Yeah."

"Personally, I mean I recognize him, we've talked, but largely about general business matters. I forget who introduced us at some fundraiser thing a year or two ago, might even be three by now. Why do you ask?" She said, and took a healthy sip. "Oh, God, does that ever hit the spot. Thanks," she said and blew me a little kiss.

I was beginning to wonder who needed tonight's possibilities more, me or Heidi? "Why do I ask? Just trying to get a handle on the guy. He's got a very difficult client, actually, I'd say she's a pain in the ass, but he's smooth, I'll give him that much, very smooth. I'm wondering if they maybe have some relationship."

"You mean like sex?" Heidi said and took another sip.

"Is there another kind?"

"God," she groaned. "If I recall, he's married, and I think he told me his wife was super religious, some born-again type," she said, then drained her glass and pushed the empty toward me for a refill. I hadn't touched mine, yet.

"I wouldn't peg him as born again," I said. Images of naked women from around the world and the vetting Royal's various sites did before you could make an "appointment" with one of his clients flashed through my mind.

"I've never met her. I think they worked together at one point. She's a techy, that was their common bond, at least initially."

"Maybe I should give her my name and have her put me on her prayer list."

"She's probably not into doing the impossible, Dev."

"Too bad," I said.

"I'm guessing she's pretty private. He's at all sorts of functions, fundraisers, political events from both sides of the aisle, city, county, and even state, but I've never seen her with him."

"I bet that was the photo on his desk, short hair, maybe kind of dull, certainly not what you'd call exciting."

"And you can tell that from just one picture?"

"Well, he looked like he was having a good time, and she looked like the type who wanted to stop anyone and everyone from enjoying themselves."

"Interesting, not. Hungry?"

"Yeah, let's eat, and let me give you a refill."

Heidi snuggled up against me and gave me a kiss without waking up. I was content to stay just where I was. The sun was up, and the digital on her dressing table said it was almost ten. Her empty Prosecco glass was next to the clock. She was going to need aspirin at some point, and I figured I would be dispatched for caramel rolls or pastry while she showered. But, that was all somewhere in the future. For now, Royal, Tony the jerk, and pain in the ass, Ashley were all far away. Then there was Tommy Flaherty….

Twenty-six

Tommy Flaherty was going to have some explaining to do in the near future. On my way home from Heidi's, I called Leo, my locksmith, and told him I needed new front and backdoor locks.

"Again? Dev, didn't we just replace those things about six months ago?"

"Was it that long ago?"

"You know if you stopped handing out house keys to every woman who let you buy her a drink, you could maybe cut down on this. I ought to put you on a monthly plan and just change the damn things every thirty days."

"You have a monthly plan?"

"I was kidding, Dev. I suppose you expect this today?"

"That would be nice. Can you do it?"

"No, to answer your question."

"No?"

"I'm up north, fishing and forgetting all about my pain in the butt clients, well until you called. Anyway, I'm out of town until tomorrow."

"Just tell me a time, Leo, and I'll be home."

"I can't be there until the end of the day. I won't be getting back in town until around four."

"I'll call you back with the lock manufacturer, so you can—"

"They're Schlage, I've changed your locks so many times I'm probably their top customer in the five-state area."

"I'll be waiting for you, Leo."

"Oh good," he said, not sounding all that sincere and hung up.

After leaving Heidi's, I did a complete walkthrough at my place. Everything seemed fine. I couldn't detect any signs that Tommy had been in this morning. Then again, until the golf shirt incident, I'd been completely clueless. Just to be on the safe side, I figured I would work from home. I fired up my computer and went online to search for deals on coffins with carved lids. I could have better spent my time looking at nude beach sites. After almost two hours, I hadn't found anything resembling Andy's missing coffin.

I watched the news while I ate a couple of hot dogs for dinner. It was "news" in name only. Nothing seemed to change. The mid-East was a mess, Putin was backing the wrong guys, Congress was grid-locked, and the Twins lost. I had a couple of beers while surfing channels for three hours then went to bed about eleven.

The police officers pounding on the front door interrupted my breakfast. It wasn't quite nine. I could see two of them standing on the front porch as I walked out of the kitchen. One appeared to be examining my porch ceiling, and the other was peering through the window of the front door. The guy looking through the window said something to his partner, but I couldn't hear what it was. They were both facing the door by the time I opened it.

"Hi, guys, what's up?"

"Devlin Haskell?"

"Yeah, what's this about?"

"Do you own a vehicle with Minnesota license number BAF479?"

"Yeah, that's it right there in the driveway, the silver Sebring, that's mine."

They looked at one another for a moment, something seemed to register between the two of them, but I couldn't tell what.

"That Chrysler Sebring?" the guy who'd been studying my porch ceiling asked and indicated my car with his chin.

"Yeah, what's all this about?" I was doing a quick mental rundown. My insurance was current. I didn't have any outstanding tickets that I could remember. One of the taillights seemed to go out from time to time, and the grill was smashed in from when I'd pulled too close to a bicycle rack I couldn't see. There was a sizeable dent in the passenger door, of course, the trunk was flat black, but I couldn't believe things were so slow they'd send two guys out to ask me about that stuff.

"Do you own any other vehicles, Mr. Haskell?"

"No, I've got enough trouble with that damn thing. What's the problem?"

"Seems to be a bit of a mix-up, would you mind holding on for just a moment while we call in?" The guy who'd peered through the window didn't wait for an answer. He just stepped back and was on his radio, trying to reach someone.

"You guys want to come in for some coffee while you're figuring things out? I got a fresh pot on."

"Yeah, I'll join you," the officer who'd been looking at the ceiling said and left his partner out on the porch to sort things out.

"Come on, I've got it on in the kitchen. So, what seems to be the problem?" I said, walking back toward the kitchen, he followed behind me.

"We've got a notice on your license number, apparently involved in some incident last night. But, the vehicle doesn't seem to match the information we have."

"Let me guess, it describes a nice car, instead of what I'm driving, right?"

The name Farrell was embroidered in gold thread just above the right pocket on his blue shirt. His silver badge was attached above his left pocket. He seemed to be studying me. I figured he was looking for a nervous reaction or whatever amounted to a guilty look. Hopefully, I hadn't given one.

"You want milk or sugar?" I asked and then remembered I didn't have any milk.

"Black is fine."

I heard footsteps coming in the front door. A moment later, his partner stepped into the kitchen. "So?" Farrell asked and took the mug I handed him.

"It's screwed up, but they still want us downtown." The other cop's name was Simpson, and he sounded frustrated.

"You want some coffee first?"

"No, I'm afraid we have to go downtown, if you want to lock up, we'll give you a lift, but we better get going." It was one of those polite sounding requests that cops make, "If you don't mind," or "would you mind stepping out of the car, please?" I'd been here before. Experience taught me to be polite back and do whatever they wanted me to do. I was going to, eventually, anyway.

"Am I under arrest?"

"Not at this stage, we'd like you to hopefully just cooperate, and then the sooner they can get this cleared up, the sooner we can get you back here to enjoy the rest of your day."

I debated calling Louie, but decided to wait and see what all this was about. "Let me just get my shoes, and I'll be right with you."

"Mind if I go with you?" Farrell said, then set his coffee mug on the counter, not waiting for an answer.

Twenty-seven

I'd been in the homicide interview rooms up on the sixth floor before, but this fourth-floor room was different, smaller, and therefore more intimate, if that was the word. Maybe it was the confined space, but the same drab color on the walls seemed somehow different. One thing remained the same. The interview room smelled of sweat, fear, and bad decisions.

"Mr. Haskell, I want to thank you for voluntarily coming down here this morning. I'm Detective Denise Dondavitch." She had probably been attractive at one time, maybe a high school cutie. But, whether it was her personal life, the profession she was in, or both, time had hardened her.

Her hair was colored a dark brown and cut in a nondescript style with a sharp part that looked more like a slit along the left side of her skull. Her eyes were a humorless grey with lots of crow's feet wrinkles around the edges. The beginnings of permanent scowl lines were already set in on either side of her mouth. If she had any makeup on, it was very little. She wore a pantsuit that had been out of style for the better part of a decade and sensible shoes. She looked to be in her early fifties, but I guessed she was probably closer to forty.

"I just have a couple of questions for you. Hopefully, we'll be able to get this cleared up, and then you can be on your way." It would have been the appropriate time to flash a quick smile, but she didn't.

I nodded. I could feel myself beginning to sweat and felt my heart rate kicking up a notch, and so far, all she'd done was introduce herself.

"Am I under arrest?"

"Not at this time," she said, which did nothing to ease my concern and, in fact, seemed to heighten my stress. "You apparently own a 2007 Chrysler Sebring, silver, I believe, is that correct?"

"Yes, well except for the trunk, right now that's flat black."

"How long have you owned that vehicle?"

"Maybe since February of this year."

"You don't remember when you purchased your vehicle?"

"No, not the exact day. It's on my title, in the glove compartment. DMV should have that information. I got it at the police auction," I said, hoping that might add a degree of credibility to the vehicle.

She flipped a page over in the rather thick file that lay open in front of her. She seemed to read her way down the top sheet, scanning information. "Do you own any other vehicles at this time, Mr. Haskell?"

"No, I do not."

"When was the last time you owned another vehicle?"

"The last time? Well, it would have been up until the time I purchased the Sebring last February. I owned an Aztek, prior to that, what a disaster. The thing was just a money pit. One time—"

There was a knock on the door interrupting me, it opened, and a guy stepped in. He looked familiar, maybe, but I couldn't place him.

Dondavitch half turned but didn't seem surprised. "Are we ready, Jerry?"

"Yeah, anytime."

"Go ahead, then and bring it up," she said then turned back toward me. "Mr. Haskell, we're investigating a robbery that occurred two nights ago. I've got the security tape loaded. If you'd direct your attention to the screen in the corner," she said and then moved her chair back so we could both watch a flatscreen TV mounted up in the corner of the room. Even watching the Twins lose while sipping a beer down at The Spot was suddenly looking a lot better than this.

"Okay," she said and the screen came to life a moment later. There was a yellow digital readout in the lower lefthand corner ticking off seconds. As soon as the video started, it began counting down; 1:59, 1:58, 1:57.

The black and white video was taken from inside a store. From the angle of the film, I guessed the camera was mounted on the ceiling and maybe fifteen feet from the front door. The front door was actually two doors.

The kind we've all been through millions of times. Metal frame doors, with full-glass panels and a horizontal bar halfway up the door that you'd push on your way out. The doors looked like they had the store hours painted on them, but since the camera was on the inside of the store, the writing on the door was backwards.

It was clearly dark on the far side of the door, and I guessed it was the middle of the night. Detective Dondavitch was studying me, probably looking for a reaction.

A vehicle suddenly backed up to the door, and a figure got out on the right side of the car, walked to the back and opened the rear door on the car. The door opened to the side rather than up toward the roof of the car. The guy tossed something out onto the sidewalk, reached into the back of the vehicle again, then turned, took a step toward the door of the store, and that's when I saw the sledgehammer. He swung it twice. The first time he hit the glass on the lefthand door, it fractured from top to bottom. The second time he swung, the lower half of the glass shattered across the floor in a thousand little pieces.

The guy reached inside, unlocked the door then picked up whatever he'd thrown on the sidewalk a moment ago. The yellow digital readout had counted down to 1:48, just twelve seconds had passed. When he stepped inside the store, he had a stocking cap pulled down over his face with eye holes cut in it so he could see.

The stocking cap had a Minnesota Wild logo, our NHL team. They probably sold over twenty thousand of the things each season, hell, even I had one. He wore a dark, hoody sweatshirt with a skeleton pattern on the front depicting rib, shoulder, and arm bones, and he had a pair of gloves on his hands with a similar bone pattern, a unique outfit considering it was summer.

The guy walked just a few feet toward an ATM that I noticed for the first time. He wrapped a long nylon belt around the ATM and cinched it tight, then stepped back and seemed to yell something.

As the vehicle moved ahead, the long belt grew taut, and a second or two later, the ATM was pulled onto its side. The guy in the hoody pushed the ATM out through the open door as the vehicle backed up. By the time he had the thing out onto the sidewalk, the driver had joined him, and together, they lifted the ATM up against the back of the vehicle then seemed to effortlessly push the ATM inside. Something seemed to flash in my brain for a nanosecond, but I lost it just as fast. The digital clock in the corner had counted down to 0:53. A minute and seven seconds to take an ATM, lock, stock, and barrel out of that retail location. The second guy slammed the rear door closed, they high-fived one another then climbed in and drove away. I noticed they left the sledgehammer behind.

"Mr. Haskell?" Detective Dondavitch asked as she turned and stared at me.

"No offense, but what? What does any of that have to do with me?"

"Jerry," she said over her shoulder. "Back that up to thirteen seconds from the start."

"Detective, I have no idea what any of this is about." The flatscreen on the wall behind her was racing back through the security video. Jerry backed up too far, then went forward too far, then slowly backed up a second at a time until just thirteen seconds had expired on the digital readout, and he froze the image. The guy in the skeleton hoody with the Minnesota Wild stocking cap had the door open and was about to carry the nylon belt toward the ATM.

"Anything catch your eye here, Mr. Haskell?"

"Actually, other than the fact that the sledgehammer is on the ground and they left it behind, now that you mention it, no. Nothing. You got a guy with his face completely covered, wearing that goofy skeleton hoody in the middle of summer. I'm guessing this happened somewhere in the city because your department is involved, but other than that, nothing catches my eye."

"Okay. Maybe see if you can read the license number on that vehicle."

I looked back at the screen, and suddenly there it was in plain sight, so obvious no wonder I missed it. My license plate; BAF479.

"Is that my license plate?"

"It would appear so."

"But how did it get there? Did they take my license plate? I'm not missing one, a license plate, at least I don't think I am."

"And you don't have any idea who that is up there on the screen?"

"No, I really don't."

"No idea how they got your plate?"

"Yeah, I have an idea, the bastards stole it. But I think it's still on my car. I didn't notice it missing. In fact, I know it's not missing, because the two guys who brought me down here, Farrell and what's his name—"

"Officer Simpson."

"Yeah, they saw the plate this morning, they saw it on my car. In fact, that's probably why Officer Simpson called in, because it didn't make any sense to him, didn't make any sense to either of them, actually, I think."

"How do you think they got your license plate?"

"How did they get it? If I had to guess, I'd say they probably unscrewed it and then walked away carrying the thing. We just watched them steal an ATM from some commercial establishment. I'm guessing they weren't really too concerned about unscrewing a license plate from the back of my car."

"Don't you find it strange that they would return it, your license plate? That they would take the time to re-attach it to your car?"

"I don't know. Maybe they developed a conscience. Yes, I find it strange, but don't limit it to just returning my license plate. The whole thing is strange. Is this the only incident?"

"Actually, it's the third reported, but the first with a surveillance tape."

"Was one of the others a little Italian restaurant over on University?"

"Yes," she said, drawing her response out as if to suggest, 'How did you know?'

"I was there for dinner the other night." Something suddenly clicked in my head. "Let me ask you something, Detective. Did you notice anything strange about that theft?"

"What do you mean?"

"That ATM is what, about five feet tall?"

She flipped a few pages from the file in front of her, quickly read down using her finger. "No, it's closer to six feet tall."

"Okay, and I don't know what it weighs, but it's probably fairly substantial. So two guys hoist the thing up, then push it effortlessly into the back of that vehicle and something that size, that long, fits without a problem?"

"It was a station wagon, and the seats were down."

"It wasn't a station wagon. Have your guy run the tape to where they tilt that thing up into the back of the vehicle."

"Jerry."

"Yeah, okay, stop it there," I said a few seconds later. "You see it, notice anything?"

"It looks like the ATM is heavy."

"Apparently not heavy enough, they got the thing out the door. But watch how they get it in the back of the vehicle."

"Okay, Jerry."

The two figures tilted the ATM against the rear of the vehicle. If you paid attention, you could actually see the vehicle drop a bit from the weight of the ATM, then they lifted it and quickly shoved the ATM all the way in, slammed the door closed, and high-fived one another.

"I don't know if you've ever loaded the rear of a station wagon, but even with the seats down, something like a heavy ATM won't slide that easily. And if there are seats in there, by the time you fold them down, you're pushing a little uphill. That isn't just any vehicle, Detective."

"I'm not following."

"Well, actually, now that I think about it, it's perfect for this kind of job. There's a large roller installed right inside by that rear door and then more rollers further along the inside. Once they had the ATM on that first roller, it was a simple push, and the thing slid into place. It would save them ten to twenty seconds, not to mention a sore back."

"And you know this how?"

"I have a client who supplies mortuaries and funeral homes. I was just at his warehouse the other day and watched them loading up coffins. I don't know how or why they took my license plate. I really have no idea why they put the thing back on my car once they were finished with this robbery. But, I'm pretty sure the vehicle you should be looking for is a hearse."

Twenty-eight

I'd actually left Detective Dondavitch on a bit of a friendly note, sipping a cup of dreadful vending machine coffee with her and laughing about some mutual acquaintances.

Now I was back at home rifling through my dresser drawers attempting to determine what, if anything, was missing. I couldn't find my Minnesota Wild stocking cap anywhere, but other than that, I'd pretty much drawn a blank for the past two hours. Leo, the locksmith, was due late in the afternoon to change the locks. He couldn't get here fast enough for my tastes. I planned to stay home and stand guard until he arrived.

My phone rang in mid-afternoon. "Haskell Investigations."

"Please hold for Mr. Baker." It was Royal's Keeper of the Gate, Marilynn, there were a couple of clicks, and the phone began ringing.

Royal picked up on the second ring.

"Hello."

"Royal, Dev Haskell."

"Yes, Dev, thank you. I've convinced Ashley to schedule a fake appointment, hopefully for tomorrow evening, if you can make it. With any luck, we'll be able to attract whoever has been following her around. It all hinges on your availability."

"Tomorrow night?"

"Yes, we'll set up an appointment at eight, if that works for you. That's always been a pretty standard time for clients."

"I'll make it work, are you going to do this at the Gresham, again?"

"No, Ashley thinks there's a better place, the Holiday Inn, out on 94. She says there are no gardens, nothing really around the place, well except for the parking lot, and it's always quiet. If our guy is out there, he should stick out like a sore thumb."

"I'll be there early, before eight, and get the lay of the land."

"I'm feeling pretty positive about this, Dev. Just one other thing, let's not have a confrontation if at all possible. We'll just get an image of this individual, hopefully a license number, and go from there. The last thing we need right now is an incident."

"Sounds fine, Royal. If I might make a suggestion, have Tony drop her off right at the front door. That might just force our guy to hurry into the lobby if he's lurking somewhere in the parking lot, or it could force him to wait in the lobby until she's finished upstairs. Either way, it limits his options and might just make him stand out."

"Good idea, I'll pass it on."

"Then, if you can just keep the two of them under control and off the hood of Tony's car," I said, half-joking.

He ignored my attempt at humor and said, "Ashley has your phone number. I'll instruct her to communicate with you by phone."

"Let's hope it works this time, Royal."

"Thank you," he said and hung up.

Twenty-nine

Leo, the locksmith, rang about half-past-four. "Yeah, Dev, I'm about fifteen minutes away, just enough time for you to shoo all those pretty girls out the door."

"I think I'll just tell them to stay quiet and lounge in a bubble bath upstairs, Leo. I'll see you when you get here."

Leo rang my doorbell ten minutes later.

"Hi, Dev," he said as I opened the door. "Step aside. I start charging you overtime at a minute past five." Then he set down a five-gallon bucket with a bunch of tools in it and took out a drill. He had the lock in the front door changed in about ten minutes and did the back door in even less time. We were sitting at the kitchen counter, sipping a couple of bottles of Mankato Ale while Leo wrote out his invoice.

"Here you go, Dev. Parts and labor, let's call it even at one-twenty, plus the beer."

"Thanks for coming over Leo. Let me just get my checkbook, how was the fishing up north?"

"Bout what I expected this time of year, not so great. Course who the hell cares, three gorgeous days out on the lake, at night you could hear the waves. How the fish are biting is almost secondary."

I wrote my check out and slid it across the counter to him.

"Thanks, appreciate it. I work with some of these youngsters nowadays, they're amazed I don't take credit cards or some nonsense about transferring funds into my account, and then there are the ones with friend pay."

"Friend pay? You mean PayPal?"

"That's it, I think. I gotta tell you, I'm glad I'm not young."

"Leo, in your line of work, have you ever done anything with ATMs?"

"You mean like at a bank? Those are contracted out to the larger firms, in fact, it's probably handled by a division of the manufacturer. Let me think, Diebold, Triton, Siemens, God, there are a lot of companies in that end of the business."

"What about ATMs in bars or stores?"

"Same thing, the manufacturer would handle it, or some company contracted by them. Some guy like me wouldn't be involved, I'm too small, and frankly, I'm not interested."

"But you know something about them, the ATMs?"

"Just what I read in the industry journals. What are you getting at? Don't tell me you're thinking of ripping off one of those things."

"No, but not far from the truth." I went on to explain the video I'd seen yesterday compliments of Detective

Dondavitch. I didn't feel the need to mention I'd been hauled in for some polite questioning.

"And they just tossed the damn thing in the back of a car and drove away?"

"Yep, the whole operation, from the time they pulled up until the time they left, took just a little more than a minute."

"Sounds pretty efficient, as far as it goes, of course, you watched the easy part, they still have to get into the damn thing."

"But, they can do that at their leisure, say in a workshop and with all sorts of tools."

"Not quite, first off often times there's some tracking device in those kinds of units. So, even if you grabbed the thing in the middle of the night, you might be on a limited time frame and, you wouldn't want to bring it anywhere that was going to be associated with you, like your workshop, a lake place, or your barn. The whole thing just sounds like a bad idea."

"How much money do those things carry?"

"In a retail position, not that much, my thought would be those things usually dispense just twenties. Probably give you a couple of options when you use them, twenty, sixty maybe a hundred-and-twenty bucks. The bills are stored in a cassette. I think they can handle up to something like twenty-five hundred to three thousand."

"Dollars?"

"No bills, so twenty-five hundred bills at twenty bucks a pop, do the math."

"Jesus Christ, five grand?"

Leo looked at me for a long moment. "You're probably not the guy I'm going to go to for my taxes, Dev. No, fifty grand."

"You're kidding."

"Nope. And the guys who did this, along with the tracking device, there might be some pretty serious dye packs in with that cash. They're set to destroy the cash and coat whoever is nearby with some serious color. That said, depending on the location, the thing might just have a couple of grand in it and none of the security devices."

"You can't avoid the dye pack?"

"Usually not, it's set on a radio frequency. Look, some idiot screwing with this stuff, the least of his problems is getting the ATM. Once they grab that cassette with the cash, if there's a dye pack, it's just a matter of seconds once its open before that dye pack activates. That's why your average idiot pretty much stays away from stealing ATMs. If they're involved, they're either plenty smart or really stupid. Odds on favorite is they are really stupid."

"And then the guy is all red?"

"Maybe, the real intent is to destroy the money, get the bad guy to just drop it. A lot of the time, in an on-site robbery, the stuff is recovered, and the bank or whoever can exchange it. The deal you're talking about, it would be pretty tough for some deadbeat to go into the Federal Reserve with thousands of dollars dyed red and ask to exchange it."

"I think you've told me more than I wanted to know, Leo."

"My advice, Dev, don't think about stealing ATMs."

"Thanks, Leo, I'll try and remember that."

"Is your check good? Can I deposit this tomorrow?"

"As long as you're first in line, it should be okay."

"Then I'll be sure to get to the bank early, thanks for the beer, Dev. Always a pleasure learning what you're up to."

Thirty

I slept soundly with my new locks installed then drifted down to the office around noon. Louie was already there.

"Hey, we're out of coffee, man," he said by way of a greeting.

"Thanks, I'll grab some on the way home. Were you in court this morning?"

Louie had a wrinkled grey suit on today, a stain that looked like spaghetti sauce was smeared across the breast pocket. It looked like he had tried to wipe the stuff off with his hand but only succeeded in making the stain larger.

"I'm scheduled for three this afternoon."

"DUI?"

"Among other things," he said, but didn't elaborate.

I settled into my desk chair, then picked up the binoculars and gave a quick scan to the third-floor apartment across the street. Unfortunately, it looked like no one was home.

"Another 'do nothing' day?" Louie asked, then closed the file in front of him, set it on top of a small stack, pulled another file off a larger stack, and opened it.

"I'm working tonight, see if we can try and catch the guy who's taking pictures of this woman and posting them on her web site."

"That's still going on?"

"I don't really have the brightest nor the most cooperative clients. They want to call the shots, but they don't really have any idea what they're doing."

"Probably should stick to what they know," Louie said and turned a page in his file.

"Yeah, the problem there is neither one of them knows all that much."

The rest of the afternoon was uneventful. I waited for the rush hour traffic to more or less die down then headed east on Interstate 94 and out to the Holiday Inn.

Royal had been right. There wasn't much around the place. It looked like ten acres of soybeans planted across the road, and the six-story building was surrounded by parking lots on all four sides. Unfortunately, the part about the hotel being quiet wasn't quite happening tonight. There appeared to be a wedding going on. Lots of folks dressed to the nines were heading into the hotel, a number of them carried gift-wrapped packages.

I had to park in the back of one of the side lots. I pulled a sport coat out of my trunk and shook some of the debris off before I put it on. I took my time walking around to the front door of the hotel. The only thing I saw even halfway suspicious was a couple in their car.

She appeared to be reading the guy the riot act while he just kept staring straight ahead.

The lobby was about a third the size of the Gresham, with no fireplace, no oriental rugs, and no fancy ceiling trim. It did have a couple of vending machines and people, lots of people. I guessed upwards of a hundred folks were milling around, waiting for the wedding to begin. I counted four guys in grey tuxedos but didn't see anyone resembling a bride or bridesmaids. I stood close to the entrance and prayed they'd all move into a banquet room soon.

My prayers were answered about seven-thirty. The crowd gradually drifted into a banquet room just past the bar. A few minutes later, the doors were closed. I took up my position in a recently-vacated wingback chair that gave me a view of the lobby along with the front of the building and waited.

Tony's car, with its dual mufflers, rumbled to the front door at about ten past eight. Actually, that seemed to make sense since Ashley prided herself in arriving late, causing the level of expectation and excitement to rise in her client and cutting down on her working time.

She stepped out of the car, and Tony rumbled maybe just twenty feet away to a parking place and pulled in. So much for subtle, apparently he hadn't learned much in the intervening forty-eight hours.

For her part, Ashley looked stunning in a very short silky dress with a wide black belt, skyscraper heels, and enough cleavage to hide a fifth of Jameson. She held a small beaded bag in her right hand. She strutted into the lobby and headed straight for the elevators in a deliberate manner, strutting in that fashion model runway walk, one foot directly in front of the other. There were only a half dozen people in the lobby, but they all stopped whatever it was they were doing and just stared as the show walked past. Unfortunately, none of them held a cellphone or anything remotely resembling a camera.

Tony rushed in a half-minute later. He took a quick look around, gave me half a glance, and a momentary sneer then made his way to the barroom. Ashley had already disappeared into the elevator.

That was about the extent of the excitement. Nothing looked out of the ordinary. The parking lot appeared to be devoid of people. Three of the guys who had ogled Ashley in the lobby as she strutted toward the elevator climbed into a yellow taxi and drove off. There were two women wearing blue blazers behind the hotel desk and me.

About twenty minutes later, the elevator door opened and Ashley stepped out. She either ignored me or didn't see me and made a beeline for the barroom. Just as she entered the bar, the doors to the banquet room opened up, and the lobby filled with a tsunami of happy, well-wishing wedding guests, quite a few of whom were taking photos. About every third person drifted into the barroom right behind Ashley.

I got up and made my way through the crowd and into the barroom. They were already standing four deep all along the bar, waving cash and credit cards as two rather harried-looking bartenders fell further and further behind. Ashley and Tony were seated down at the far end of the bar, scowling at the growing crowd. They sat just below a flatscreen that was playing one of those reality music talent shows.

It took me some time to make my way through the crowd, but I finally got to them.

"I think we might as well try and leave. This looks like it could go on for the rest of the night," I said.

"What the hell is this shit?" Tony said, then took a long sip from his pint glass. I noticed his fingers were red like he'd painted them.

"What do you think it is, it's a damn wedding, Jesus," Ashley snapped.

"There's no way we're going to be able to spot anyone with all this going on," I said. I had to raise my voice and lean into Ashley's shoulder so she could hear me. When I did, I caught a brief whiff of her perfume, very nice.

"Did you get him? See anything, anyone?"

I shook my head. "Plenty of folks watching you as you made your entrance, but no one with a camera or cellphone."

Four women at the table closest to Tony had placed their arms over one another's shoulders and were squeezing together for a picture. A fifth woman was standing in front of them, holding her cellphone and seeming to take an inordinate amount of time focusing, to get everything just right. She'd caused two people to lean far back in their chairs, so she had room to take the picture. By this time, the smiles on her subjects had begun to appear pasted on. She remained oblivious.

"I think you should get out of here, Ashley. That guy could be taking pictures of you right now, and we'll never even see him. It's like open season on you in here," I said.

There were more than a few guys staring at Ashley as they waited in line for drinks. Tony was looking at her, and you could sense the wheels slowly beginning to turn in his one-watt brain.

"You think he's in here?" she asked Tony.

"Course he is, and the son of a bitch has all the cover he needs. Great move asshole," Tony said, sneering at me then slammed his empty pint glass on the bar.

"Tony's right," I said, ignoring the last part of his comment. "I think we should get you out of here, Ashley. With all these people, the guy could be right in front of us, and we'll never know it."

She seemed disappointed but nodded, and we headed toward the door, Ashley was in front of me, parting the waters as she strutted through the crowd. Guys stepped aside and stared at her while Tony brought up the rear and attempted to intimidate guys with his scowl; it didn't seem to be working.

Although the lobby had a number of people in it, compared to the barroom, it almost felt empty. We were halfway across the lobby when a shorter guy caught my attention. He seemed to take a long look at Ashley and then ran out the door. By the time we made it outside, the guy was kneeling down and seemed to be waiting for us. He was just a few feet from the door holding his cellphone out, getting ready to take a picture.

Ashley stopped dead in her tracks and moaned. I thought we might have our man, unfortunately so did Tony.

"What the hell, you see this shit?" Tony half yelled and pushed me into Ashley as he jumped in front of the guy with the cellphone.

It all happened rather quickly. As Tony reached for the guy, I heard screams from a woman and two teenage girls who were standing off to the left behind us. Apparently, they'd been posing for the photograph.

Tony's reach was interrupted by the guy grabbing his wrist, then flipping Tony up, over his shoulder, and slamming him down onto the concrete. The guy hung onto Tony's wrist then turned, and we heard a definite crack. Tony's scream was cut short by the elbow he received to the side of his head. When the guy let go, Tony dropped like a limp rag, unconscious onto the sidewalk, and his head bounced off the concrete a couple of times.

"You want some of this," the guy said and looked directly at me.

"No sir. I don't know what got into him. Are you all right?"

"What the hell is it with you city types?" he said, then walked over to the woman, I guessed his wife, and two teenage girls, probably daughters and said, "Come on, we're checking out and heading home." He glared at me while he held the door then followed them into the lobby.

Tony was still out cold lying on the concrete. Ashley was kneeling next to him, slapping him lightly back and forth across the face saying, "Come on, Tony, come on," as she phoned 911.

Thirty-one

The paramedics seemed like nice guys. They collected some general information from Tony. He didn't realize he'd be getting a bill for somewhere between twelve to eighteen hundred for their time. The cops were nice, two suburban guys from Woodbury. They talked to Tony and Ashley then a handful of witnesses, myself included.

Tony's story of an assault from behind along with his demand that they send in the SWAT team to hunt the guy down and shoot to kill quickly fell by the wayside. Ashley was purposefully vague when asked what she and Tony were doing at the hotel. I'm not sure, but I got the distinct impression that some prior offenses might have come up on the computer, and that seemed to change the course of the officer's questions.

From what I could determine, the five witnesses, myself included, had no idea who the other guy was, and all seemed to agree he had just been defending himself from an unprovoked attack. The officers left while the paramedics were placing Tony's arm in a sling.

One of the paramedics told Ashley it would be substantially less expensive if she drove Tony to the ER, but she shouldn't wait until tomorrow to do it. At the end of it all, Tony was groggy on painkillers, Ashley looked ready to kill, and a large part of the wedding crowd had drifted out with drinks in hand to see what all the excitement was about. I decided to flee the scene.

"Well, it sounds like you'll probably be heading to the hospital, so I think I'll just get back to the office." I took a couple of steps back just in case she tried to hit me with her little handbag.

Tony looked over at me and grinned idiotically, "Wow, guess we showed him, huh?" He had a bruise on the left side of his face. His eye was swollen almost closed and gaining a decided purple cast. Red fingers wiggled out from the edge of his sling.

"Really? You mean you're leaving me with this?" Ashley hissed.

I couldn't tell if by "this" Ashley was referring to just Tony, or to the entire situation. Right now, I didn't really care.

"You're a competent woman. I'm sure you'll be able to handle things, Ashley. You know your way to the hospital, right? Let's talk tomorrow. Okay?" I said and began walking backward to get some distance between us.

Ashley just stared until one of the paramedics asked her something, and she had to turn and face him, at which point I beat a hasty retreat around the corner and ran to the safety of my car.

Thirty-two

I drifted into the office a little after ten the following morning and immediately placed a call to Royal Baker.

"Yes, Mr. Haskell, he was hoping you'd call," Marilynn said in a no-nonsense tone. "Let me put you through immediately."

I waited while the phone clicked then finally started ringing. Eventually Royal picked up after a half dozen rings. "Royal Baker." His usual sing-song pleasant tone was noticeably absent.

"Royal, Dev Haskell."

Royal waited for a long moment before he said anything. I started to wonder if we'd been disconnected.

"Yes, Dev, I heard from Ashley this morning, she was quite upset. Apparently, she had to take Tony to the emergency room last night. What in the world is going on? I know we had an agreement that there was to be no confrontation, but this fellow was taking pictures of Ashley, then he and his cohorts assaulted Tony while you, apparently, just stood idly by content to simply watch the entire incident not bothering to offer the least bit of assistance."

"That's what she told you?"

"I got it straight from Ashley early this morning. My understanding is Tony was still sedated. They're concerned about a concussion resulting from a number of blows to the head. His arm was fractured in the process of defending Ashley, just in case you were interested."

"Defending?"

"Thank God he was there. Lord only knows what would have happened if he hadn't been," Royal said.

"Let me tell you something, Royal. Any conditions resulting from the beating he received are his own damn fault. There was a guy, just one man and rather small as a matter of fact. He was there taking a picture all right, but he was taking a picture of his wife and two daughters. Ashley wandered into the shot, oblivious as usual. That petty thug, Tony pushed me out of the way and attempted to assault the poor guy. Based on the results you just relayed, I'd say he picked the wrong person to try and push around. By the way, multiple blows to the head? I don't think so, I saw it, Tony got hit on his thick skull just once."

"That doesn't seem to jive with Ashley's rendition."

"There's a surprise. Royal, no offense, you seem like a nice enough guy, but I've just about had it with your client, Ashley and her tag-along heavy, Tony. Why don't I just get an invoice to you, and we can call it even."

"Under the circumstances, Mr. Haskell, I'm inclined to agree with you. Last night was extremely traumatic for Ashley."

"Well, she picked the place. Tony attempted to assault the wrong guy, and Ashley seems to have her head permanently up her ass, I don't know what else I can tell you."

"I'll await your invoice," Royal said and hung up.

I turned my chair toward the window, picked up the binoculars, and scanned the building across the street for any sign of life. Add another disappointment to my day. Just for laughs, I went online and scanned eBay and Craigslist for coffins. I didn't come across anything that sounded like the ones Andy Lindbergh was missing. The way things were going, I determined this might not be the best day to buy that winning lottery ticket. Andy Lindbergh phoned me after lunch.

"Dev, Andy, I'm just checking in."

"Hi, Andy, if you're wondering about those coffins, I really don't have any news. I've been checking online, looking at items for sale, but haven't seen anything resembling them."

"I was afraid of that."

"Has anything else gone missing on your end?"

"No, at least not that we've been able to determine. Well, except for your friend, Tommy."

"Tommy?"

"Some vicious flu thing, he's been told to stay home for a week. Apparently, it's a pretty contagious strain.

Certainly don't need something like that raging through here."

"And he's out for a week?"

"Yeah, at least a week, doctor's orders. He sent a friend over to get his collection files. He's been working from home. What a trooper."

Some other terms sprang to mind. I didn't want to ask Andy for an address, and I could only hope Tommy had purchased a phone and was actually making some collection calls.

"You didn't happen to meet his friend, did you?"

"As a matter of fact, I did, nice enough guy, I guess. Wouldn't want him dating one of my girls, but he picked up Tommy's files and rumbled out of here in some souped-up chariot.

"How has it been working, the collections?"

"Well, it's an uphill battle, a very steep uphill battle. I guess I don't have to tell you. But, he has been making some progress. Say, will you excuse me? I've got another call coming in I've been waiting for, let me get back to you," Andy said and hung up before I could respond.

I drummed my fingers on the desk, thinking. An ATM is stolen and driven off in a hearse with my license plate on the vehicle. Leo told me about the dye packs that would explode destroying the money, staining the robbers, and now Tommy Flaherty has some strange flu bug and has to work from home. I needed to find out where he was living.

Thirty-three

I placed the call and crossed my fingers. "Hi, Lissa, please don't hang up."

"Is this Dev Haskell?"

"It is?"

"Do a lot of people do that, hang up on you? Or is it just your funny way of getting a girl's attention? Gee, a second phone call from you, and after all this time. To what do I owe the pleasure?"

"Actually, I was calling to see if you could give me Tommy's phone number or better yet his address."

"Tommy?"

"Yeah, your brother. I just wanted to check in with him, make sure everything is going okay. I'm hearing good things from his boss, but I didn't want to bother him at work. I'm thinking maybe meeting him somewhere, you know for dinner or something."

"I've got a better idea, why don't you and I meet for dinner, just for old time's sake. Never know what might happen. Besides, it's the least I can do after you arranged that job for Tommy."

"That's really not necessary. I wouldn't want to put you to any trouble."

"Believe me, Dev, it's no trouble at all, the pleasure will be all mine, well and maybe yours too, once we've had dinner. What does tomorrow night look like for you?"

I didn't have anything scheduled for the next week. "Tomorrow night? I think I could move some things around. Do you want me to pick you up, or would you like to meet somewhere?"

"Let me pick you up, Dev, say around seven."

"You sure?"

"I insist, just give me your address."

"I'll be working. You mind meeting me at my office?"

"Your office?" she said, not sounding all that sure. "Well, okay, yeah, I suppose, just tell me where."

I gave her the address then said, "It's just kitty-corner from The Spot bar. Randolph and Victoria."

"I'll be there around seven, let's make it a memorable night."

The term "memorable night" suggested my luck might finally be changing. I picked up the binoculars and scanned the building across the street again, nothing, a virtual dead zone. If my luck was improving, it hadn't improved by much.

I got on the computer and cranked out my invoice to Royal. I charged him the minimum amount, made a point of mentioning there was no charge for the botched incident last night, where Tony had his ass handed to him then closed by wishing him the best of luck in his search for whoever was stalking Ashley. After that, I phoned Heidi.

"Hi, Heidi, I'm wondering if you can help me."

"You know my answer, Dev, I'm not posting bail, and I'm not driving ninety miles to some godforsaken place just to give you a ride back to town."

"Are we having a bad day?"

"No, but based on past experience, I'm just stating some facts, Mister."

"Okay, okay, actually, I wondered if you had a home address for Royal Baker. I just wanted to send him a thank you card, and I thought it might seem a little more personal if it arrived at his home."

"Really? God, when did you become so considerate?"

"I can do nice things.'

"I know you can, but it's usually things like giving me way too much Prosecco or getting a room at an expensive hotel."

"Yeah, well, those are nice things, too."

"Hang on, I'm just clicking on that file. Okay, here we go, yeah he lives on the River Boulevard, you got a pen?"

"I'm all set to write it on the wall."

"Huh?"

"Just kidding, Heidi, go ahead."

She gave me the address, then asked, "How are things going on your case with Royal and his client?"

"It's closed, not as neatly as I would have hoped, but I'm finished, signed off, so to speak." I didn't feel the need to tell her about Tony getting slapped around, Ashley lying and really pissing me off, me quitting, and Royal more than likely disgusted with the whole bunch of us. We chatted briefly, then she had to run.

I figured I would just deliver my invoice to Royal's home, so it would be waiting there for him this evening. I'd had more than one instance where my invoice had been conveniently lost in the office mail until I had to threaten to take the client to court.

Thirty-four

Royal lived in a three-story red brick colonial with black trim, a glossy red front door, and a view of the Mississippi River bluff just across the street. A constant parade of joggers, walkers, and bicycle traffic drifted along the river bluff. I debated for a moment about just dropping my invoice through the mail slot in the door. Instead, I knocked using the brass lion's head knocker just above the little plaque that read No Solicitors then waited.

The door opened about three inches a minute later. I could see the brass chain linked from the door frame to the back of the heavy door. A short woman, maybe just five feet one or two peered out at me with soft brown eyes.

"Yes."

"Hello, my name is Dev Haskell. I have a letter I'd like to drop off for Royal Baker." I said and extended my envelope toward her.

"What's this about?"

"I've done some work for him, his company actually. It's just my invoice."

"Haskell? Are you that private investigator Royal told me about?"

"I guess so."

She closed the door, and I heard the lock slide off the hatch, the door opened again, this time wider. "Won't you come in, Mr. Haskell?"

"Please, call me Dev, and I don't want to be a bother showing up like this unannounced."

"No, it's not a bother at all. In fact, I'm glad you stopped by. Please, please, come in. I'm Royal's wife, Gemma," she said, then opened the door wider so I could step inside.

The entry was about eight feet deep and had large black and white floor tiles that looked like marble. There was a leaded glass door with a leaded glass window on either side leading into the main part of the house. I followed Gemma into a large foyer with a white staircase running along one wall up to the second floor. What looked like a cozy living room with a fireplace was on one side of the foyer, and a larger, more formal living room with an even larger fireplace was on the other side.

"I just put the kettle on for some tea, would you care to join me?"

I wasn't the tea type but smiled and said, "I'd love to."

She was the same woman I'd seen in the photo on Royal's desk, only much more attractive in person. She had a nicely toned figure, dark blonde hair styled and cut to just above her shoulders. She was dressed in an attractive pair of shorts with a matching blouse and sandals with woven leather straps. I followed her toward the rear of the house, past two large, ornately framed landscape paintings and into a large kitchen with lots of windows.

"Do you take milk or sugar?"

"Maybe a little sugar," I said, hoping it might kill the tea taste.

"I'll let you doctor it," she said and pushed a silver tray across the marble countertop. The tray held a small silver pitcher of milk and a small silver bowl full of sugar cubes with a set of tongs resting on top of the bowl. "Please, have a seat," she said.

I settled onto a comfortable stool then grabbed the mug of tea she had placed in front of me. I dumped four sugar cubes into the mug, hoping it would help.

"Care for some pastry?" she said and opened a white bakery box on the counter.

"No, thanks," I replied and then studied her from the back as she busied herself at the sink for a moment.

"So," she said, turning around to face me. "Royal mentioned you were doing some investigative work for him."

"Yes, we spoke this morning, and I told him I would be sending an invoice. I thought it might be better if I just dropped it off here. I was going to leave it in the mail box," I explained then took a sip of tea. It wasn't all that bad.

"I understand things didn't quite go as planned the other night."

I didn't mean to, but I must have given her a puzzled look.

"Royal received a call about five-thirty this morning, that Ashley person. I suspect they may be rather close," she said, then paused for a moment and sipped, letting that last statement just hang out there, maybe waiting for some reaction from me before she continued.

"I think she phoned from Regions hospital. Something about an assault? Photographs? I could hear her voice as she screamed through the phone, but I couldn't make out exactly what she was saying. All I know is Royal appeared rather upset once he got off the phone." She sipped some more tea and seemed to smile to herself, apparently finding some comfort in the incident.

"Well, a bit of a misunderstanding, I'm afraid."

"Did someone assault her?"

"No, it was actually him, I don't know, her boyfriend or husband. I'm not really sure what their relationship is."

"Too bad," she said, making it sound like it was too bad Ashley hadn't been the victim.

"Would it be alright if I left this with you, Gemma?" I said and pushed my invoice across the counter toward her.

"I'll be happy to see that Royal gets it, and I'll let him know we had a little chat. So, you're off the case. It's finished, you caught your man."

"Not exactly. I'm off the case, more or less by mutual agreement. As far as finished or catching anyone, I'm afraid we didn't. Part of it isn't adding up, but for the life of me, I just can't seem to figure out what it is."

"Do you do a lot of this kind of thing, Mr. Haskell, investigating?"

"Yes, I'm a private investigator."

"So, you're experienced."

"Somewhat, I've been doing this for a few years. It's actually not like the crazy things you see on TV. Usually it's pretty boring."

"Do you carry a gun?"

"On occasion."

"Well then, I had better remain on my best behavior," she said and smiled.

I got the sense it was time to leave. "It was very nice to meet you, sorry to interrupt your afternoon and thanks for the tea."

"Thank you for drinking it. I gather it's not your first choice."

"It was very good."

"I'll show you out," she said and headed back toward the front door. "Do feel free to stop again, Mr. Haskell," she called as I was halfway down the front walk to my car, then she closed the door before I had a chance to turn and respond.

Thirty-five

I didn't hear from Royal or anyone else for that matter until late in the afternoon. "Haskell Investigations,"

"Dev, honey, it's Lissa, just making sure we're still on for tonight."

"Yeah, seven, you sure I can't pick you up or just meet you somewhere?"

"Afraid of my driving?"

"No, just trying to make it easy for you."

"I'll call you when I'm about a minute away. You can just run downstairs and hop in."

We hung up, and I wondered if it was just a throwaway phrase, or did she know my office was on the second floor?

Lissa phoned me five minutes before seven. "I'm downstairs waiting," she laughed and hung up. She was parked right in front of the door, sitting behind the wheel of a snappy red BMW convertible with the top down, looking sexy and gorgeous.

"Wow, nice set of wheels."

"Just one of the many little pleasures in life," she said, raising her eyebrows suggestively at "pleasures." "Come on, hop in, baby, and let the fun begin."

She had always been just a little on the wild side, but then again, it had been a few years since I'd seen her. She was wearing a short skirt and a sheer top that left nothing to the imagination, even while she was just sitting behind the wheel. Her hair was shorter and a bit lighter than I remembered, and windblown from her drive over with the top down. She looked great as I slid into the seat and buckled up.

"So good to see you, Dev. You haven't changed a bit. If anything, you look even more delicious. It's been way too long," she said, then leaned over and gave me a long kiss on the cheek. A wonderful perfume engulfed me, and I inhaled deeply. She lingered just long enough to rub her hand up and down my inner thigh a few times, then pulled back and seemed to take a deep breath. "Whew, you certainly haven't lost any charm, Mister. Come on, let's get started, I've been thinking about this for the past twenty-four hours, and I can't wait," she said then pulled away from the curb.

We hadn't driven more than a block when she leaned toward me and said, "Now listen, I've made reservations at the Levee, and I'm paying. I don't want to hear any argument from you. It's the very least I can do."

The Levee was located along the Mississippi and was one of the more trendy places in town, which was probably one of the reasons I'd never been there. The other reason was that it cost an arm and a leg.

"You know, Lissa, a cheeseburger and a beer would suit me just fine, you're almost making me feel kind of guilty. I appreciate the thought, but I'm sure we'll have a good time wherever we go."

"You're right on that count. We are going to have a fantastic time, memorable I think is the word I used, remember? And we're going to start with drinks and dinner on the Levee. Now, not another word, you just sit back and enjoy the view," she said, and with that, she casually reached down and hiked her skirt up exposing more than just her thigh. She turned toward me, ran her tongue slowly back and forth across her upper lip, and smiled seductively. My luck was definitely changing.

We pulled into valet parking, and the two kids parking cars just stood there speechless and stared at her as she climbed out from behind the wheel. The one holding her door open followed her with his eyes as she strutted around the front of the car and into the restaurant. You could actually see his eyes move from left to right with every step she took.

The place was filled with all sorts of trendy people wearing a lot of very expensive casual clothes. My nineteen dollar jeans and the St. Paul Saint's shirt might have been the cheapest outfit there, but then again, I was with the hottest woman in the place, and she was buying.

I saw two guys sitting at the bar looking like off-duty lawyers or bankers. They were wearing handmade woven Italian loafers and no socks. They stared at Lissa as she walked up to the hostess, then they leaned in toward one another and began to conspire, probably trying to figure out how I rated. Either that or they were going to finish their drinks and then run out and buy a couple of St. Paul Saint's shirts.

"Good evening, how are we doing tonight?" the hostess said. I pegged her at barely eighteen years old and probably the envy of all her friends because she was working here.

"Just fine, thank you. We have a reservation, Flaherty," Lissa said.

The girl checked a computer screen for a moment, "Oh yes. You requested a table outside, didn't you."

"That's us."

"For three. If you'll just follow me, we're all ready for you."

They were off in a flash, and I had to catch up. Three? I wondered if Tommy was going to show up. God, I hoped not, things were off to a great start. The two swells without socks watched Lissa as she moved her delicious figure in that incredibly short skirt toward the rear door.

Our table overlooked the river on the outside deck about fifteen feet above the water. It was the perfect evening, not a cloud in the sky, warm, but not too hot with just the hint of a breeze. Way above us, a bald eagle slowly circled, working its way downriver. He seemed to circle a few times directly over our table, probably checking Lissa out. A couple of boats worth about six figures motored past as two racing skulls rowed downriver in time to the coxswain calling the pace.

I pulled the chair out for Lissa to sit then sat down at a ninety-degree angle to her with my back to the door.

"Can I get you something from the bar?" a waitress asked. She was dressed all in black: slacks, shirt and a long apron.

"I think I'll start with a virgin cosmopolitan," Lissa said and then looked at me.

"What do you have on tap?"

"Oh, Dev, no beer tonight, don't you like bourbon?"

"Well yeah, but I was thinking a beer—"

"Do you still have that sampler you used to do?" she asked the waitress.

"Yes, the Taste Treat? We do have that. You're not driving, are you?" She only half-joked.

"Dev, you've got to try it, six different bourbons, you taste them, and it's amazing how different they really are, come on, besides I'm driving, at least the car," she said then shrugged and grinned.

"I suppose. Yeah, I could go for that."

"Give him your six best bourbons," Lissa said.

The waitress nodded then said, "We'll get those drinks over here to you in just a moment."

"You'll just love it, amazing how different they all are," Lissa said.

"A virgin cosmopolitan?"

"I can still pretend, of course, who'd know better than you?" she said and I felt her foot running up my shin as she smiled.

"Sounds nice."

"You just wait, Mr. Haskell, I might have to be arrested, did you bring your handcuffs?" she said, flared her eyes and glared.

I had to swallow to keep my composure. "Say, Lissa, the hostess said three, who's going to be joining us?"

She glanced anxiously toward the door. "Well, I hoped to get a drink or two in you before I mentioned it."

"What? Your brother, Tommy?"

"No," she said, drawing the word out and sounding more than a little mysterious.

"Well who?"

"It's my sister, Candi."

Thirty-six

That didn't make any sense. "Candi? Your sister who told me to never, ever, call her again just a couple of weeks ago? The same sister that filed a restraining order against me and threatened to castrate me when we all went our respective ways?"

"Well, Dev, you were dating the two of us at the same time, and neither Candi nor I was aware of it. At least until that night you called my name out at a rather intimate moment with her, you idiot," she said and laughed.

"But Candi?"

"Dev, we had a talk, Candi and I. She was really hurt at the time, but she's moved on, we all have. Anyway, I happen to know she's coming to apologize and well, look, I'll just let her tell you the rest, but I have a feeling you might like what she has to say."

"Do I have to check her for weapons?"

"She just might enjoy a thorough search by your hands. I know I would," she said, then ran her hand along my forearm.

"All right, and the cosmopolitan?" A server asked. It wasn't the woman who took our order, and Lissa raised her hand. "And I guess the bourbon taste treat would be for you, sir."

"That's right." I said as she placed a wooden tray in front of me with six large shots of bourbon resting in little holders. The shots all looked like they were doubles.

"I told you you'd like it," Lissa said and stroked my arm again, then she raised her cosmopolitan and said, "Here's to a very memorable night." She sipped, flashed her eyes at me over the rim of her glass, and then smiled.

Between the bourbon, the stories, the stroking of my arm, and the kisses she kept giving me, I lost track of time. It was dusk by the time Candi arrived. Lissa stood and hugged her, then gave her a big kiss and whispered into her ear.

Candi giggled, then looked down at me and shrugged. She bent down and gave me a couple of very firm kisses on my cheek then ran her tongue over my ear.

Lissa just smiled, then reached under the table and stroked my leg.

"Can I get you something from the bar, Ma'am?" our waitress asked.

"I'll have exactly what she's having," Candi said and pointed at Lissa's almost empty glass.

"I better have another, too," Lissa said. The waitress looked at me with a bit of a question. I still had two shots to go, and like I'd said, they were doubles. "Sir?"

"Sure why not, we can help out if it's too much," Lissa said

I was feeling no pain, and by the time I was thinking it might not be the brightest idea, a fresh tray with six more shots had been placed in front of me.

The two of them seemed to be toasting something about every thirty seconds. The weather, the river, old friends, new adventures, memorable nights. We'd all raise our glasses, the sisters would take a sip and seemed to smile at one another. By this point, I was pretty much downing the entire double shot. I was vaguely aware I was having trouble pronouncing the occasional word. A while later, I was aware I was having trouble thinking about which word to use. The next thing I knew, the two of them had me linked arm in arm, and they were pouring me into the back seat of Lissa's convertible.

We were all laughing, and Candi slapped me hard across my rear, then gave me a solid push into the back seat. I remember thinking, if I could just close my eyes for a moment I would probably be okay.

"Come on, let's go party," one of them screamed, they both laughed as the car drove off and I more or less passed out.

I'd no idea how long I'd been asleep, it could have been five minutes or five hours. One of them was tickling me, pulling me up into a sitting position. I was vaguely aware of my shirt being unbuttoned. I was pushed forward as someone pulled it off. I remember thinking, 'isn't this nice, they're putting me to bed.' But I was still sitting in the chair. Only it wasn't a chair, it was the back seat of Lissa's convertible, and I was suddenly lying on my back with my feet up in the air as my jeans were yanked off my legs an inch at a time.

"Good enough?" a voice said.

"No, the deal was all or nothing," came the reply, then someone tugged my boxers off. I figured the least I could do was help, but beyond that, I was incapable.

"God, he's actually laughing."

"We'll see how long that lasts."

"Dev, Dev, come on honey, time to get out of the car. Come on baby, time for the memorable night we've all been waiting for."

"Oh my God, I think we got him too drunk. He's still out of it."

I opened my eyes and attempted to say, "I am not", but I think it just came out as a garbled mumble. Candi grabbed my hand, then pulled and motioned me forward with her free hand. "Come on, baby, come on, this is going to be so much fun, just think of it, sisters."

Lissa was behind me, pushing me out of the car and grabbing my ass.

I was wearing a stupid smile and black socks.

I have a vague recollection of their taillights fading into the dark night as Candi knelt backward in the passenger seat and lifted her top to expose herself. "See, this is what you're missing, you big dumb jerk."

Then I fell down, or maybe I just passed out.

Thirty-seven

When I woke, the first thing I noticed was I had one hell of a headache. I had apparently gotten sick, oh, and I was naked. My clothes were nowhere to be found. I had no idea where I was, and it was still dark out.

I was on a lawn or at least a field where the grass was cut. I walked up a small rise, and there was the Mississippi river with the lights of downtown shimmering across from the far side. I recognized the Wabasha Bridge, and instinctively knew I wasn't that far from home, maybe three miles. The distance wasn't a problem, but the no clothes had the potential to present some difficulty.

There were a couple of stationary garbage cans in the parking area behind me. I made my way to one of them, getting sick again along the way. There wasn't that much left to come up so, it was more a case of the dry heaves, but still not fun.

The trash container had a locked door on it, but I could see the garbage can with the plastic trash bag inside holding lots of trash, food wrappers, and a number of disposable diapers. I reached in and began to empty the trash bag, one handful at a time. I threw everything out onto the ground then reached back in the bag for the next choice item.

Once I had emptied the better part of the trash bag, I unhooked it from the outside of the can then gradually worked it out of the can and the locked container. I dumped the remaining contents onto the ground, tore a hole in the bottom of the bag and slipped it on over my head.

It was wet and cold against my skin, with some distinctly unpleasant odors wafting up around my chin. The bag hung down below my knees. I began heading in the general direction of my house as the plastic trash bag rustled with each step. Three cars passed me on the Wabasha Bridge, each one slowed down for half a moment, no doubt to get a better look, then sped up and raced across the bridge, getting as far away from me, as fast as possible.

By the time I'd made my way to the far side of the bridge, there was a squad car waiting for me. Its lights were flashing, and two officers were leaning against the trunk of the car. They looked like they were having a casual conversation, and my arrival was interrupting. A second squad car was following me, maybe twenty feet behind, moving forward slowly and just keeping pace with me.

"Hi, can we help you?" one of the officers leaning against the trunk asked. I could see his partner trying not to laugh.

"Yeah, I've been attacked and robbed. I'd just like to get home."

That wiped the smiles off their faces.

"Why don't you get inside the squad car, and we can talk?" said the guy who had been trying not to laugh. He opened the rear door for me.

I walked over and slid into the back seat, the plastic trash bag rustled all around me. As I went past him, he grimaced at the smell. They both climbed into the front seat, seemed to sniff, and immediately lowered their windows. The squad car that had been following behind me waited just a minute or two and then took off.

"Can you tell us what happened?"

"Yeah, sure. I was with some friends tonight, we got separated, and a couple of guys jumped me, took my wallet, my clothes and left me in that park across the river there. I had to get this stupid trash bag to cover me. It was the only thing I could find. Hey, look, guys. I got some pals on the force, they could vouch for me if you want to check with them. But I don't feel so great, it's been kind of a long night, and I'd like to go home."

"What's your name."

"Haskell, Devlin Haskell. I'm a private investigator. I know Lieutenant Aaron LaZelle in homicide, Detective Manning in there as well. I was working with Detective Dondavitch a couple of days back on an ATM robbery. I office on Randolph Ave, across from The Spot bar, and I live about a block past the Cathedral. So it would only take you about three minutes to drive me home, and I'd really like to get there. I'd be forever in your debt."

"Have you been drinking, sir?"

"I think someone might have slipped one of those date rape drugs into my drink."

They shot a glance at one another, then the guy behind the wheel said, "Do you have any identification?"

"Identification? I'm wearing a trash bag for God's sake. A used trash bag."

The guy in the passenger seat smiled and looked out the window. The guy behind the wheel said, "Call it in, ask them to send a DMV image."

They got on the radio and talked to someone. Then asked for my name and address, I guess in case there were two guys with my name. An image of me popped up on their dashboard computer a few minutes later. It was my driver's license photo, and based on the way I looked on their computer, I figured I would probably be arrested for war crimes.

As I sat there in the back seat, I could feel something either dripping or crawling down my chest. I wasn't sure which it was, and so I just sat there and waited. They crackled back and forth with someone on the radio, most of which I couldn't understand, but I think someone had called Aaron LaZelle on the phone. It was well before sunrise, so I'm sure he was pleased.

"Would you like us to take you to Regions Hospital to get checked out?"

"Thanks, but if you guys could just take me home, that would be great."

"Okay, Selby Avenue you said?"

"Yeah," I gave him my address, and we took off.

We were parked at the curb in front of my place in a matter of minutes. "Thanks again, fellas, I really appreciate it."

"You sure you're okay?"

"Nothing that a hot shower and some sack time won't cure, maybe ditch this trash bag."

"Might be a good idea." Something came across their radio, and the guy in the passenger seat jumped out and opened the door for me.

"Stay safe," I said as he climbed back into the car, they were off with the lights flashing a moment later. I was just remembering that I'd had the locks changed the other day and hadn't replaced the spare key I had hidden when I saw a pile of clothes on my front porch. It was my jeans, Saints t-shirt and boxers. For a moment, I almost felt like forgiving the Flaherty sisters. Almost.

I pulled the trash bag off over my head, gathered up my clothes, took the keys out of a pocket in my jeans, and unlocked the front door. I held my clothes out in front of me, so they didn't come in contact with whatever was dripping and crawling on my skin and made a beeline for the bathroom upstairs.

My reflection in the mirror looked dreadful, and I didn't want to contemplate what some of the stains and debris clinging to my flesh were. I took a very long, very hot shower and used up the better part of a bottle of shower jell.

It was almost five in the morning, and I was ready to climb into bed when I remembered one more thing I had to do.

After the sixth or seventh ring, Lissa answered, even though she cleared her throat a couple of times, she still sounded raspy and groggy.

"Hi, Lissa, mistake. Very big mistake." I said, and hung up. I placed a call to Candi, but she didn't answer, so I left a message saying the same thing. Then I climbed into bed, pulled the sheets up, and drifted into a very sound sleep.

Thirty-eight

I was up just before noon and phoned Aaron while I sipped my first cup of coffee, I ended up leaving a message apologizing for the predawn police phone call. I phoned Louie next and did the same thing, left a message, this one saying I needed a lift to the office if he was available. I waited for two more cups of coffee then called a cab to take me down to the office. When I got there, Louie was sitting at his picnic table reading a file.

"How long have you been here?"

"All morning, I've got a one-thirty court appearance," he said.

"You didn't get my call? I was hoping I could be able to scam a ride from you this morning."

"A ride? I thought that was your car out front. I just figured you were over at The Spot for a liquid breakfast. What's up?"

"You don't want to know," I said then proceeded to tell him all the gory details.

"Sounds like the two of them had the whole thing planned right from the get-go."

"Gee, do you think? If two guys did this to some woman, they'd be sentenced to a couple of years."

"I suppose, on the other hand, it seems pretty obvious what they intended to do. If you tried to press charges, they might be able to make the case you were thinking with the wrong head, or just ran off into the dark, and they couldn't find you."

"If only I'd been able to do that last night."

"What do you intend to do?"

"Do? Probably nothing. I don't want to waste much time trying to get even. I phoned both of them once I got out of the shower and shouted something like 'Big mistake' into the phone. They'll hopefully stress out wondering what I have planned, and that's good enough for me. The last thing I need is to get into some pissing contest with either one of them."

"Wow, that almost sounds wise, go figure."

My phone rang just as I was reaching for my binoculars.

"Haskell Investigations."

"Devlin Haskell, please."

"Speaking."

"Mr. Haskell, this is Gemma Baker, Royal's wife. I hope I'm not interrupting."

"No, no, not at all. What can I do for you?" I said and set the binoculars back down.

"I'm wondering if we might meet. I think I'd like to hire you."

"Is everything okay?"

"Actually, that's what I'd like you to find out."

"Is someone threatening you and Royal?"

"Actually, this is just for me, in fact, I'd really appreciate it if you didn't mention this call to Royal."

"All right, I could probably stop over this afternoon if that would work?"

"No, I would prefer not to meet here."

"Do you know Nina's, it's a coffee shop up on Selby and Western?"

"I do know it, and that would be just fine, would say, three-ish work for you?"

"I'll see you at three, Gemma, thank you for calling."

"And not a word to Royal about this, please."

"I won't mention it. I'll see you this afternoon."

"Thank you," she said and hung up.

"One of your dates from last night, calling to see if you're available this evening?" Louie asked. He was in the process of putting his laptop into his computer bag and getting ready to leave.

"No, amazingly, it was actually someone who wants to hire me."

"Maybe don't sound so surprised when you're talking with her," Louie said and then headed out the door.

I scanned the building across the street with my binoculars. I monitored some college girls waiting for the bus on the corner then drifted my gaze back to the apartment building. Nothing was shaking in either direction. I made my way up to Nina's a half hour before my appointment. Gemma was already there waiting.

"Gee, and I thought I was early," I said, sitting down.

"May I get you a coffee, Mr. Haskell?"

"No thanks. Please, call me Dev. What's this all about? Are you all right?"

"Me? Oh yes, in fact, I've haven't felt this positive in quite some time."

I waited a few moments letting that statement just hang out there, hoping she might come across with some follow up, maybe elaborate. She didn't.

"So, you mentioned you had something you would like me to investigate and, you don't want me to mention it to your husband."

"Exactly," she smiled and nodded.

"Would you care to let me know what I should be investigating?"

"What? Oh, why yes, how very silly of me. I'd like you to investigate Royal of course."

"Royal?"

"Yes."

"What do you think he's done?"

"Not only *what* he's done, Dev. But, what he is *continuing* to do. His 'relationship' if I can use that word, with this Ashley person."

"She's a piece of work, alright. I've only interacted with her a few times, none of it was very pleasant. I can tell you this, my dealing with Royal and Ashley was strictly on a business level, and that is certainly the way

Royal seemed to conduct himself the few times I was involved." I hoped that put her at ease.

She smiled and gave a quick glance around the room. "Dev, do you know anything about me?"

"Anything about you? Well, no, not really. I know you're married to Royal, obviously. I think you met through work, and I may have heard that you have a strong religious faith."

"I majored in chemistry and computer programming at the university. I was one of Royal's early programmers. I'm very aware of his subtle charm. In fact, no one is probably more aware than me. As to a strong religious faith, that's a line Royal likes to spread around. I think the term he usually uses is 'religious fanatic.'"

I just nodded and wondered where this was going.

"Obviously, having been there at the beginning, I'm entirely aware of what Royal's business is all about. After all, I helped set it up. As to the religious aspect, Royal likes to mention that thinking it probably keeps me out of the way. I'm no more religious than the next person. I suppose he told you we have separate bedrooms?"

"No, he didn't mention anything like that."

"Interesting, usually he does. We don't, by the way. We still share the same bed, at least on the nights he's home."

"What is it you would like me to investigate?"

"Do we need to sign a contract to swear you to secrecy?"

"No, not unless that would make you feel more comfortable."

"No, that won't be necessary. If I'm wrong about you, I doubt a piece of paper would matter anyway. I have the sense I can trust you, Dev, I hope I'm not disappointed."

"You can trust me."

"I intend to file for a divorce. Before I do that, I'd like documented proof that Royal is having an affair or perhaps even multiple affairs. I'm fairly certain he's been involved with Ashley for quite some time, I suspect others as well."

"What makes you think that?"

"Mmm-mmm, everything, and nothing. The phone calls taken into the next room, the late-night showers when he comes home or the perfume I smell if he doesn't shower. I think you'll find his meetings with Ashley are usually at some hotel, and they're not sharing a table in the dining room."

"And you said you helped establish his business?"

"I think what I said was I helped set it up. I'm familiar with the nature of his 'clients' business affairs and the, shall we say, security services he provides. Let's face it, Dev, the advent of personal technology, and individuals like Royal have brought the world's oldest profession to the brink of legitimacy."

"And you want what, exactly? Receipts, times, dates, room numbers?"

"I want confirmation that will stand up in court. I was wondering if pictures wouldn't help."

I nodded then said, "Do you have any idea when these private get-togethers might be happening?"

"You mean like all those incessant *board meetings* that seem to go on until eleven or twelve o'clock? Please, spare me. Yes, he has me pegged as so naïve that he calls ahead. More than once, he's actually phoned from a hotel. I followed him once with the intent of confronting the two of them, but that Ashley woman had some dreadful character with her, and he threatened me."

"How did he even know who you were?"

"Actually, I approached him. I saw him arrive with Ashley. I guess he's her pimp or something. That criminal sat drinking in the bar, waiting for her little tryst with Royal to be completed. I simply walked up to him and demanded to know what room she was in. I never actually mentioned Royal."

"And?"

"And he threatened to kill me if I didn't leave, then he showed me a gun. I panicked and ran out to my car."

"Was this guy about my height, dark hair, not too bright, obnoxious attitude?"

"I'd say that sums him up."

"I know who you mean. His name is Tony. We've crossed paths a few times. In fact, he's one of the reasons I'm not working for Royal any more. I'm not sure of the relationship he has with Ashley, husband, brother, maybe boyfriend, but he fancies himself a lot smarter than he actually is."

"He behaved like an absolute criminal, imagine. I had no doubt he would have murdered me given half a chance."

"Did he know who you were?"

"Other than a dejected spouse, no. He didn't seem to put Royal and me together. Royal never mentioned the incident, so I have no reason to believe that Tony person even mentioned it to him."

I nodded. "Putting you and Royal together would require at least two consecutive thoughts, and I don't believe thinking has ever been Tony's strong suit."

"So, you'll do it? Get me the proof that will stand up in court?"

"I can try. What I'd like from you would be a heads-up call when you get word Royal will be home late. I can try and take it from there."

"I can do that, but I won't know where they're meeting."

"Let me worry about that. What kind of car does Royal drive?"

"A dark blue one, it's a Mercedes, he's very proud of it."

"Do you know the model?"

"Oh, I should, I mean I see it every day, but I never pay attention to that sort of thing. I can tell you the license plate."

"You can?"

She nodded and smiled, "It's one of those personalized plates, it says Royal, R-O-Y-A-L," she said, spelling it out

"Did Royal ever mention anything to you about images placed on Ashley's site?"

"So that was Ashley? Oh, interesting, I thought as much. He mentioned something briefly, but never divulged any names. I didn't think much of it, he has clients from all over the world, so I just never put it together that she was actually the individual involved."

"You'll let me know the next time you receive one of his 'working late' calls."

"I definitely will. It's been happening on an almost weekly basis lately and once in a while twice a week. You should be hearing from me in the next few days. He usually calls to alert me in the late afternoon, between four and five."

"I'm sorry you're going through this, Gemma, let's see if we can't bring it to a conclusion for you."

"I'd like that," she said, then we exchanged thank you's and went our separate ways.

Thirty-nine

I was sipping coffee at my desk the following morning while I looked out the window waiting for the mailman. I'd been expecting a check for the past week, but despite promises from the client, I hadn't seen anything. Andy's call interrupted my worrying.

"Dev, did you check out craigslist this morning?"

"You beat me to it. I was just about to do that. Did you find something?" I said and reached over to turn on my computer.

"It's our black walnut special order. There's a photo of the thing posted online as big as day."

"You're sure?"

"No doubt about it, the family crest is carved on the lid, and there's a brass plaque just below the carving where the name was to be engraved."

"Does the ad have contact information?"

"Yes, but it's one of those anonymous email addresses, you know a bunch of numbers plus a symbol and then, at Gmail dot com."

"Give it to me," I said. I wrote the email address down and then repeated it to Andy.

"Yeah, that's it."

"Here's what I suggest, I'll contact them, offer to purchase. I've got a handful of nondescript email addresses like the one you just gave me. Depending on where they're located, we'll get the local authorities involved. Anything on the other two coffins?"

"Milo, anything on those other two?" Andy was probably standing in the doorway of Milo's office while Milo searched. "No, nothing so far."

"I might hold off for a bit, just in case the other two show up, then we could possibly go after all three. What's the latest on Tommy Flaherty, is he okay?"

"No, heard from him again yesterday, he's still struggling with that flu bug."

Yeah, he's probably trying to get the red dye off his skin and failing miserably, after my episode with his sisters I could only hope.

"Let's touch base in an hour, Andy," I said, and hung up.

The craigslist image of Andy's coffin looked like the thing was lying in someone's living room. It had been photographed on a carpet with a dark couch and a flatscreen TV in the background. There was a beer can resting on an end table alongside the couch. The room looked like any other living room in probably millions of homes across the country.

The ad itself was extremely brief and purposely vague. 'All wood coffin. Dark wood, hand-carved, best offer, must sell.'

I liked the "must sell" part, like whoever it was couldn't keep up with the payments, or maybe they wanted a coffee table in their living room instead of a coffin. I didn't come across anything resembling the other two missing coffins, so I called Andy back about an hour later.

"Andy, Dev."

"Milo couldn't find anything resembling the other two coffins," Andy said.

"I didn't see anything either. I've got that ad on your hand-carved piece up in front of me now. The ad reads like they don't have the slightest idea what the value is of this thing."

"Yeah, I'd say they're out to lunch. They don't even mention that it's black walnut and already lined. Actually, in a way, that may be a good thing. Hopefully, that eliminates any of our staff. They'd all be aware of those features and point them out."

"Here's the deal, I think I should send them an email, making an offer. What did you say this one was worth?"

"The price to our client was fifty-five hundred. Just the way this ad is written, I think they don't have a clue."

"I'm gonna send them an email offering a grand. I'll add some wording suggesting I'll raise the bid if I have to because I really want the thing. What we need to do is find out where this is so we can get it back, and we also want to nail their ass."

"Go for it, man, and let's see what happens."

I sent off a reply to the craigslist ad. "Very interested, can pay $1000. Please let me know before you accept any other bid." Then I sat back and waited.

Forty

I was still waiting the following afternoon when Gemma phoned.

"Hello, Dev, this is Gemma."

"Hi, Gemma, did you hear anything?"

"As a matter of fact, I just hung up with Royal. He'll be late as usual due to a board meeting, and he told me not to wait up for him."

I looked at my watch, it was a little after four. There was a good chance if I hurried, I might catch Royal leaving the office in his Mercedes with the designer plates. "Gemma, thanks, but I had better run if I hope to follow him."

"Happy hunting," she said and hung up.

I was cruising through the parking lot at Royal's office twenty minutes later. After just a few minutes, I spotted his car parked up close to the front door. I pulled into an open space, three rows back and waited.

I needn't have hurried. I was still there two hours later, thinking maybe the guy really did have a board meeting when he suddenly strolled out to his car. It was the tail end of the rush hour, and Royal drove out of the lot, onto the interstate, and headed east. He took the Geneva Ave, Highway 120 exit and pulled into a hotel parking lot within sight of the exit. I drove past the hotel, then made a U-turn through a corner gas station, circled back, and pulled into the hotel lot.

I didn't see Royal, but I spotted his car parked up toward the front. I figured he might be checking in, or at least still en route to his room, so I hurried across the lot and took a couple of photos on my cell with his license plate and the hotel entrance prominently displayed. Then I climbed back in my car and waited.

It must have been a slow night because it was a good half-hour later before the next car pulled into the lot, Tony and Ashley. I heard them before I could see them with Tony's muffler giving off its throaty rumble. I couldn't help but wonder how much the neighbors appreciated that. The little I knew of Tony, I was sure the thought never even occurred to him.

They parked about three spaces away from Royal's car, and as they walked past, Tony made a comment. They both looked at the Mercedes. Ashley nodded and said something back that got both of them laughing.

She was wearing a short black skirt that barely covered her rear, a silky black blouse, a wide sequined belt with a sparkly buckle, a string of pearls, and black knee-high boots with stiletto heels. If there was a board meeting, she was going to be the best dressed person in attendance.

Tony looked his usual idiot self in jeans and an olive drab t-shirt with an image on it. I was pleased to see his left arm was still in a sling. I was pretty sure I knew the drill, Ashley would head to the elevators and Tony would head for the bar. I waited another five minutes just to be sure then went out to take a couple of pictures of Tony's car.

Given the close proximity, I was able to photograph both vehicles with the second vehicle appearing in the distance. Would these stand up in court? Probably not, but it was a start.

After forty minutes, I ventured into the lobby. The bar and restaurant entrance was just past the main desk. I peeked in and caught a glimpse of Tony sitting alone at the bar. Most bars offer pull-tabs, a state sponsored gambling option. For a couple of bucks, you buy a card and pull off the tabs to see what, if anything, you've won. Tony appeared to be in the process of filling a plastic cheeseburger basket with losing pull-tab cards and drinking a beer. I figured he already had to be down by at least fifty bucks.

I walked up to the front desk. A young woman with a blue polyester blazer and a wide smile said, "Good evening, how can I help you?"

"I'm supposed to meet a friend, Royal Baker. I believe he checked in this afternoon. If you could give me his room number, please."

"I'm sorry, I can't give you his room number, but I can give you his phone extension, and you can reach him on our house phone right over there," she said and pointed to the phone on a table between two comfortable looking wing back chairs. "Let me get that extension for you. You said the name was Baker?"

"Yes, Royal Baker."

"Oh yes, here it is," she said, then wrote a four-digit extension number on a business card and slid it across the counter to me.

"Thank you," I said and walked over and took a seat next to the phone. Unfortunately, the extension was 1015, and there were only eight floors in the hotel. I'd hoped the extension could have translated to a room number, but no such luck.

Still, I did have the phone extension written on a hotel business card, and it might help if it could be married up with a credit card receipt. I pretended to talk on the phone for a moment, and then when the girl at the front desk turned around, I made my way out the door and back to my car.

Tony and Ashley were the first to leave a couple of hours later. Ashley looked more than a little disheveled and maybe high. Tony looked unhappy, and although I couldn't hear him, I could sense by the body language he wasn't pleased.

Ashley stopped at the rear of the car to make some remark as Tony was about to get behind the wheel. I took a couple of shots of them just as Tony stormed toward her. Ashley took a step or two back just as he grabbed her by the arm, then marched her to the passenger door, half threw her into the seat, and slammed the door.

He chirped the tires backing out of his parking place, picked up speed through the parking lot, then screeched his tires as he pulled onto the road and accelerated out of sight.

Royal exited maybe a half-hour later. He looked nicely groomed. Like maybe he'd taken a shower and gotten cleaned up. There seemed to be the slightest spring in his step, and he was whistling. I took a couple of shots from the front seat of my car then waited until he exited the parking lot before I phoned the hotel.

"East View Lodging, how may I direct your call?"

"Yes, would you connect me with Mr. Royal Baker, please?"

"Sure, one moment, please. Oh, I'm sorry sir. It looks as if Mr. Baker recently checked out."

"Checked out?"

"Yes, sir, I'm afraid so."

"All right, thank you very much."

So much for Royal's board meeting.

Forty-one

I went online first thing the following morning. There was an email message waiting for me regarding the coffin. It simply read "We have a better offer." I sent a response back that said, "I'll pay you $100 more." I forwarded both emails to Andy then called him.

"Hi, Dev. I've got both of those up now. They just came through."

"I'd be surprised if they had another response, even at the give-away price I offered, that's still a grand and then what would the market even be for a coffin on craigslist."

"What if they come back and tell you someone offered four or five grand?"

"I'm sure they're going to come back and tell us someone offered more, they may not even mention a figure. I'll tell them I can have guaranteed funds, a cashier's check, or even cash, and I'll pay five hundred more than whatever offer they have, something like that. In fact, I may just wait a few hours, send another reply sounding like the anxious customer and say I need it due to a death in the family, and I'll pay five hundred more and I'd like to pick it up tonight or tomorrow."

"Think they'll go for it?"

"I think it's probably the only offer they have. I know someone I can call who'll go with me. I'll send him in. We'll contact whoever the local authorities are and nail this guy."

"Good."

"The more I think about it, Andy, the more I'm willing to bet we're going to find the other two coffins with this individual."

"God, if only it would be that easy. Keep me posted."

"My pal Tommy Flaherty still out?"

"Yeah, had a phone message waiting for me when I came in this morning. Must be one hell of a flu bug, poor guy."

"Yeah, must be. I'll keep you posted," I said, then hung up and put a call into Gemma Baker.

"Gemma, it's Dev Haskell."

"I was hoping you'd call, how did things go last night?"

"That depends on your point of view."

"In other words, it's all true, isn't it?"

"Unfortunately, that would seem to be the case." I related what I knew, how Royal had a room, Ashley and Tony arrived a good half hour after Royal, Tony waited in the bar, they left some hours later and then Royal left about a half-hour after that.

"I called the hotel as he was driving away, asked to be put through to his room, and they told me that he had just checked out."

There was a long pause on the other end of the phone before Gemma cleared her throat then said, "Well, I guess that's the kind of proof we needed."

"Not exactly."

"How so?"

"Well, I have shots of them leaving, although they're from pretty far off. I have shots from the parking lot with both their cars in the same image, but so what? They could just say they were both there for a beer and a meeting. Plus, with Ashley's guy Tony there, his presence actually adds some credibility to that denial."

"So, what do you suggest?"

"Just that we stay vigilant, let me know when another one of Royal's working late calls comes through, and I'll see if we can't get a little more creative."

"That's it?"

"I'm afraid so, we're really dependent on their schedule at this point. I can tell you this. My experience is that quite often with a series of these images the contest never actually makes it into court. The evidence you'll have becomes so overwhelming in Royal's eyes that he'll agree to whatever settlement you demand."

"That doesn't sound like Royal."

"Guilt can be a pretty persuasive argument."

"That really doesn't sound like Royal."

Forty-two

My email response on the craigslist ad came through in the early afternoon. "We have an individual ready to purchase, but you sound so nice. What offer can you make?"

I forwarded the response to Andy then called him.

"God, they sure sound like they're working you. What a bunch of jerks, if you were legit, trying to get a coffin for a loved one, this is what they do? Make you twist in the wind for a couple more bucks? If I didn't want to nail this idiot before, I sure as hell do now."

"I'm going to call my pal, see if he can join me and we'll get this thing shut down tonight or tomorrow. I'll offer to pay five hundred more, cash and tell them I need to know today."

"We're available to verify the item once you get it. I've got a file right here on my desk from the shop that built it, invoices, specifications, the family crest design, photos of the finished piece, everything. The way they're operating, I'd say there's a good chance it hasn't even crossed their mind to remove our barcode. Keep me posted, Dev."

I hung up with Andy and placed a call to Luscious Dixon. Luscious had been a defensive end on three different NFL teams, all during the same preseason. He never played as much as a minute in any game, which seemed in itself to be an NFL record of sorts. He had a number of issues, apparently one of them being anger management, which helped to explain the felony convictions and his habit of quickly becoming a marketing liability to whatever team he signed with. If I remembered correctly, I think his record was seventy-two hours with the San Francisco 49ers. Ultimately, it was decided Luscious drew the sort of attention the entire league was better off without. The anger issues, felony convictions, and the bad-boy profile made obtaining regular work somewhat difficult in the new caring and more sensitive NFL. He answered my call after a half-dozen rings.

"Mmm-mmm," he grunted.

"Luscious, it's Dev Haskell."

"Dev, what trouble are you in now?"

"Actually none, surprisingly. Hey, I'm working a case, and I was thinking, you might be the perfect guy to help me out, you busy?"

"Never too busy for you, Dev. What you got?"

I gave Luscious a brief description of the situation. Then I said, "So basically, all I'm looking for is someone to drive a rented pickup truck and show up with the payment. I'll be right behind you, somewhere, probably have a cop there, too, and we'll nail this bad actor.

Shouldn't take more than a few minutes once we get to wherever we pick the thing up."

"You know you can count on me, Dev. When you thinking all of this is going down?"

"I'm dealing with this nitwit on email. I'm going to try and set it up for sometime tomorrow. That work for you?"

"I'll make it work."

"Perfect, I knew I could count on you, Luscious."

"You just let me know where, Dev, and I'm there."

I got back online and sent my response. "Willing to pay $500 over your best offer, but need to send my son tomorrow to pick it up. I can pay cash. Please forward details."

My response came through about five minutes later. "Have an offer for $3000. If you can go to $3500 we have a deal. Will forward directions once we hear from you."

I waited a half-hour then responded. "God bless you, this is just wonderful. My son will have the cash payment, $3500. Must have this to the mortuary by end of day tomorrow. You are in my prayers, Lucille."

I got an almost immediate response. "Sold. Glad to be of service. Lucille, my mother would be so happy. Our home is difficult to find. Your son can meet me at the Denny's restaurant on I-94 and Manning drive at 10:00am. Let me know if this is a problem."

I forwarded the emails to Andy again and called him.

"God, the guy almost sounds legit," Andy said.

"Yeah, well except for the line about his mother, and then there's the line about the home being difficult to find. I'm guessing there'll be at least two people checking my guy out. I know this place, the Denny's, not a lot of places to hide and cool your heels out that way."

"Anything I can do to help you?" Andy asked.

"Only by staying away. Whoever this is, there's at least a fifty-fifty shot they'd recognize you or one of your employees. They had to be familiar enough with your operation to get this out of there in the first place. By the way, anything else missing?"

"No, not a thing. It's strange, these three things and then nothing else."

"In other words, the moment you learned things were missing, you tightened security and probably shut down whatever they had set up, whether you knew it or not."

"Yeah, maybe."

I didn't mention the fact that Tommy Flaherty hadn't shown up almost since the day this caper was discovered. Now, more than ever, I felt like I owed it to Andy to nail whoever was behind this, and I had a pretty good idea who that was.

Forty-three

I phoned Luscious and told him we were on for seven tomorrow morning.

"You gotta be kidding me, in the morning?"

"Yeah, Luscious, amazingly there's a seven in the morning, too."

"Man, I'm not at my best that time of day, Dev.'

"Look, you just be ready to go, I'll pick you up, by the way, Luscious, I plan on bringing doughnuts."

"Now you're talking, what kind?"

"What kind do you like?"

"Chocolate's my favorite. I've always been a big fan of the sugar ones. Course the ones with the jelly inside and them chocolate ones filled with cream is good, too."

"Luscious, how 'bout I bring you some of each, then you're going to drive that truck to a Denny's, and you can probably get a big breakfast there, if you're still hungry."

"Seven in the morning?"

"Yep, and with all those doughnuts, so you just be waiting for me, okay."

"All right, I guess I'll be there, Mr. Dev. You can count on me."

"I am, Luscious, I am."

Next, I phoned Detective Dondavitch. Someone else answered her phone, and she came on the line a minute or two later.

"Haskell?"

"Yeah, Detective, you got a minute to talk?"

"Maybe just, what's up?"

"Remember that ATM deal from a while back, you ever get that thing figured out?"

"No, fact is, it's growing cold at this stage. Not much to go on other than that security tape with your license plate."

"I think I might have something, possibly." I told her about the missing coffins and how one turned up on craigslist. My suspicions about the other two and then, how Tommy Flaherty had called in sick for the past week.

"He said the flu, this time of year?"

"Yeah, with a guy in his early twenties, it strikes me as odd, and like I said, the guy has a history."

"Spell his last name for me?"

As I did, I could hear her clicking on a keyboard. "Here he is," she said a moment later. "Not exactly what you'd call successful. He certainly would be a candidate, and you think he stole coffins?" she said, and half laughed. "What in the world did he think he could do with those?"

"I guess sell them. There seem to be more and more coincidences with this guy, and I've learned over the years never to trust a coincidence. Once I heard about the flu bug that really put the spotlight on him. The coffins, possible access to a hearse, he's suddenly missing work for almost a week. Anyway, we're going to pay cash theoretically tomorrow morning. I'll be meeting the person at a Denny's out on I-94 instead of their home. You interested?"

"It's more than we've got now. Let me make some calls, that's two jurisdictions over."

"I'll forward all my emails to you, read through them, and make your own decision, but I'm thinking we can nail this guy, and there's an outside chance we'll get that ATM heist as the icing on the cake."

I pulled in front of Luscious' building a little before seven the following morning. Luscious was nowhere in sight, but I was a few minutes early and didn't panic. His building was a five-story brick affair that reminded me of a high school homecoming queen twenty years on who had stopped caring about her appearance, shabby around the edges, but a hint of what had once been.

The double door entry had the name Graceland painted in an arc of gold script letters with black shadows, then the address 391 nestled beneath it. The building predated Elvis arriving on the scene by fifty years, and you had to wonder if it was coincidence or was the name changed as a tribute. Either way, it was more than a little ironic that the likes of Luscious Dixon lived in a building with the name of Graceland.

At ten minutes after seven, I climbed out of my car and rang the buzzer next to the name L. Dixon. I rang it off and on for the next three minutes. Finally, a grumpy sounding voice barked, "This better be worth it."

"Luscious, it's Dev, come on, you're late."

"Do I have to?" He whined like a six year old.

"Yes, you have to, come on, you promised me, and I got a lot riding on this. Besides, I got all these doughnuts down here just waiting for you."

"Doughnuts?" he said, sounding a lot more awake.

"Yeah, and lots of them."

"What kind?"

"Let's see, some chocolate ones, a bunch of sugar-coated doughnuts, chocolate with cream filling, and the ones filled with jelly. You don't want them, I guess I could give them away to these guys coming down the street."

"Don't you do that. I'll be down there in just one minute."

It was more like five minutes, but he was there. I could feel the vibrations as he thundered down the stairs from three flights up, and suddenly he was standing at the door.

"Where those doughnuts you promised?" he growled when he saw me standing on the front steps empty-handed.

"Come on, I've got a whole box of them for you in the car."

Luscious opened the passenger door and pushed the seat back as far as it would go before he gingerly climbed in. My car creaked and groaned as it leaned to the right at about a forty-five-degree angle.

"You know, Luscious, if you don't mind, it might be more comfortable for you in the back seat, and besides, that's where the doughnuts are."

He moved pretty fast for a big man, and he looked a hell of a lot happier stretched out across the back seat. The white box from the bakery had a red plastic band wrapped around two corners to keep it closed. Luscious set the box on his lap, pulled the band off, and then slowly opened the top of the box as if it contained treasure. He took a deep breath once he lifted the lid, and his eyes opened wide as he gazed on three rows of assorted doughnuts. There was an even dozen of the things, at about two thousand calories each, a virtual cardiac train wreck just waiting to happen.

"Which one of these you want, Dev?" he asked as I pulled away from the curb.

"I already had breakfast, Luscious you just help yourself. Have 'em all if you feel like it."

"Mmm-mmm, which lucky one gets to go first?" he said, then took a massive chomp out of one of the chocolate cream doughnuts, closed his eyes, and smiled.

We were at the truck rental place over on University maybe ten minutes later. It took a couple of minutes to talk Luscious into leaving the doughnut box in the back seat and just choosing one doughnut to bring into the office.

"You lock this car up good and tight, Mr. Dev. I don't want some worthless bastard running off with these."

"It's locked, Luscious. They'll be safe. You can keep an eye on them from out of the window of the office."

We walked in the door, past aisles of rental equipment to a counter in the back of the place. Two guys were sitting behind the counter next to cash registers talking about fishing. They each had a steaming mug of coffee sitting in front of them. They seemed to size up Luscious as he wolfed down a jelly-filled sugar doughnut and then gave me the nod.

"What can we do for you?" the older of the two asked.

"Need to rent a pickup for the day."

"Not a problem," he said and clicked a couple of keys on a laptop then turned the thing toward me. "Just fill out that form, I'll need your license and insurance number. Thirty-five dollars a day, one hundred miles at no charge. After that, she's thirty cents a mile."

"Not a problem." I turned toward Luscious, licking his fingers in an effort to capture the last bit of jelly and sugar. I angled the laptop toward him and said, "Luscious, you mind filling this form out for them?"

Luscious took his time licking his fingers then said, "I ain't got no driver's license, Dev, it's been suspected."

"Suspected? You mean suspended?"

"Yeah, that's the one."

The two guys behind the counter didn't even blink.

"I'll fill this out," I said and spun the computer back toward me, trying to make the best of a bad situation.

When I was finished, the guy spun the laptop back around, scanned my driver's license, clicked a couple of keys then said, "You want our rider insurance? Forty-five bucks, don't mind me saying it might not be a bad idea." He glanced quickly off to the side, indicating Luscious who was staring out the window and keeping a watchful eye on my car with his box of doughnuts in the back seat.

"Yeah, I suppose I better. Thanks."

Forty-four

On the way over to the back lot to get the pickup, I handed Luscious my car keys and said, "I'm going to pull around to the front. Then I want you to follow me in my car. We're just going around the block, and we'll switch so you're driving the pickup. You'll follow me out to the Denny's restaurant and go inside. They'll be looking for you, maybe you can grab some breakfast, maybe you can't, we'll just see. Now don't worry, I'll be watching you, but you won't be able to see me."

"Cool."

"Yeah, and one more thing. I got this envelope of cash for you. You can show it to them if they ask, but don't give it to them. Got it?" Then I handed a thick manila envelope stuffed with tens and twenties over to him.

Luscious nodded and stuffed the envelope into his front pocket.

"They're gonna take you to get the coffin...."

"Say what?"

"The coffin, you know, like for a funeral. Now...."

"That's what I thought you said, Dev. I don't know, man, this is starting to sound like some bad luck shit."

"It's what we're buying. It's not like they're gonna ask you to climb in the thing and test it out, besides, you wouldn't fit. You just follow them, do what they say, but do not give them that money, got it? Because they'll run with it, and if they take that money, then you won't get paid by me. I'll be following you. So even if you don't see me, I'm there."

"You're buying a damn coffin?"

"If you'll remember, I already bought a big box of doughnuts, and they're sitting in my car right now, just waiting for you. You can put them with you in the truck when we go around the block here, or if the coffin really bothers you, I'll ask one of those two guys in there to help me, and they'll eat all the doughnuts, your choice, Luscious."

He seemed to weigh his options for a moment, then nodded and said, "Okay."

"Good, now follow me around the block. Once we're out of sight of this place, we'll switch vehicles."

I pulled the rented pickup out of the back lot and around to the front where Luscious sat waiting behind the wheel of my car, eating another doughnut. The two guys from the rental office had gotten off their stools behind the counter and were watching us through the front window while they sipped coffee from their mugs. We drove around the block without incident. I didn't have the courage to ask Luscious why his driver's license had been suspended or for how long. We switched vehicles, and Luscious carefully placed the doughnut box on the passenger seat next to him.

"Now, just remember, Luscious. You hang onto that envelope with the cash until they take you to wherever that coffin is. They ask you anything, you just say you're doing this for your mother, her name's Lucille."

Luscious looked at me strangely and said, "Her name is Delice."

"Yeah, but we're going to trick them, so you just pretend for today that it's Lucille, got it? And remember, you can show them, but don't give them that envelope."

"Till I see that coffin, I got that part, Dev. I got it good."

"Then let's be off, Luscious. You'll have those doughnuts in the truck to tide you over until you get to Denny's and can order breakfast," I said, and then we headed east on I-94 and out toward Denny's.

Rush hour was winding down, which meant everyone on the road was able to do about sixty or sixty-five with no real problem. That is, everyone except Luscious and me. I tried to speed up to the rate traffic was moving, but Luscious, following behind me, kept the pickup at about forty-five miles per hour. He just oozed down the far right lane all the way out to Denny's. He was traveling so slow that he screwed up folks trying to merge onto the interstate as well as all those trying to exit off. I lost count of the number of horn blasts he got as folks shot past and gave him the finger.

We made it to Denny's with just a couple minutes to spare. I figured that would just make Luscious look like he was responsible, then again, appearances can be deceiving. I slowed slightly, as I approached Denny's then waved my arm in the direction of the restaurant, hoping Luscious took his attention off whatever doughnut he was eating just long enough to make the turn.

He slowed and pulled into the parking lot, not putting his blinker on until after he'd already made the turn. I traveled maybe a half mile further down the road to a Holiday Station, drove through the line of pumps, back out onto the road, and pulled over onto the shoulder. We were about a five-minute drive from the St. Croix River and the Wisconsin border.

Forty-five

My phone rang about ten minutes later.

"Haskell, Dondavitch here. This guy you're working with, would he easily be the largest guy in this place? Oh, say by maybe close to four hundred pounds? He just had a couple of plates of scrambled eggs set down in front of him, and he was eating doughnuts from a box while he was waiting."

"That's my man, Luscious."

"Luscious? Why would anyone ever call him that?"

"No, that's really his name, he was in the NFL." I didn't feel the need for any more detail. "Is there anyone with him?"

"No, but then again, maybe he ate them."

"Shit, they're late," I said and worried they might have caught on and wouldn't show.

"I'm thinking they might just be playing it safe, and they're maybe watching from somewhere for some kind of set up."

"Anyone look like they might fit the bill?" I asked.

"More than a couple of folks, which probably means they aren't the ones. Where are you? Please don't tell me you're hiding in the men's room."

"No, I'm down about a half-mile, sitting on the shoulder of the road across from the Holiday Station."

"Do me a favor, get off the shoulder, and pull into the lot, park in front of the place. Anything happens here, I'll call you."

That sounded a lot better than sitting out on the shoulder. I pulled into the lot, then backed into a spot that was furthest from the door and waited. My phone rang about five minutes later, I answered on the first ring.

"Haskell, I think we got something. Someone just came over, and she's talking to him."

"She?"

"Yeah, looks like she might be your type, could be considered nice looking if you like 'em slutty." I heard a couple of laughs in the background.

"You with someone?"

"Another lady, we're just a couple of moms stealing a morning coffee break. Okay, she just sat down in the booth with him."

I had a hunch. "Has she got a pretty nice figure, light blonde hair?"

"Yeah, but that probably describes half the women in here, including the one across the table from me. You give this guy something in a manila envelope? He's showing it to her, opening it up, cash I'm guessing?"

"Yeah, he's supposed to hang onto it, show it to her, but not hand it over."

"Looks like he's following directions, and she seems happy enough."

"I might know that woman he's talking to. She's the sister of the guy I suspect on your ATM heist."

"So, that would be good news," Dondavitch said.

"Yeah, well, at least for you. It might also mean that idiot is still covered in red dye from the ATM, or he would be there talking to my guy. If she's who I think she is, she may be driving a red BMW convertible."

"God, but you do get around."

"I can only hope it's her."

"Your guy is pulling that bakery box closer to him. He had two enormous platters of scrambled eggs in front of him. He's pushing the one away and starting in on the second. Jesus, I can't believe it."

"What?"

"Just the amount of food he's going through. It doesn't look like he's missed too many meals."

"He's just getting warmed up. How'd you like to have him join you in the shower or rolling over on you at about three in the morning?"

"I'm telling you there wouldn't be room. She's waving away the waitress with coffee. He's guy is picking up his eating pace. Might be getting ready to go." Then I heard her say, "Put a ten on the table for our coffee and let's wait in the car."

I could hear background noise, but Dondavitch wasn't talking. I wasn't sure what was happening until she came back on, some minutes later.

"We're in the car, waiting. There's a pickup on the far side of the lot with rental info painted on the door, that your guy?"

"White truck with green lettering?"

"That's the one."

"Then, that's my boy."

"We're gonna sit until they come out, I'll call you when we have a direction. You're off the shoulder?"

"Yeah, I'm backed into a space in the lot."

"Just stay there until we know what direction they're going. Don't leave the lot. They could be heading your way."

"Got it."

A few minutes later, she said, "Looks like they're heading back onto the interstate. God, I hope they don't go east into Wisconsin." A minute later, she said, "Okay, good, they're heading west, back toward town."

I turned my car on, waited for some guy to creep past me trying to decide which one of the four empty spaces he should pull into. Naturally, he chose the one right next to me. He came to a complete stop, waited a moment before slowly backing up and cutting my exit off. He sat there for a moment, apparently wondering how to put his car back into drive.

I honked the horn at him a couple of times which only seemed to add to his confusion. Finally he moved forward into the space, pulling in about a half-inch from the side of my car. I cranked the wheel and pulled out of the lot, then accelerated, picking up speed in an effort to catch up.

I needn't have worried. Luscious was setting the pace. I picked up the phone and talked to Dondavitch. "I'm just coming down the entrance ramp heading West on 94. How far off are you guys?"

"Probably about ten feet in front of you. What's with that pickup truck? Is he pedaling the damn thing, or can it only do about thirty?"

"I should have warned you, he's the original cautious driver."

"Jesus Christ, if we drive like this all the way back to St. Paul, we'll qualify for overtime. It'll be dark out by the time we get there at this rate."

"Anyone give him the finger yet when they sped past?"

"I'm about ready to do that myself. Oh, by the way, you were right, your lady friend is driving a red BMW convertible. Flaherty, Lissa Flaherty. I got her up on the screen now, doesn't seem to have any priors."

"God, I'm wondering if she'll go to her house, or maybe her sister's?"

"You know the family?"

"Know of them, don't really know them anymore."

"Hey, you were right. Someone just gave your guy the finger," she laughed.

We drove along the interstate, heading back into St. Paul. Eventually, we passed all the downtown exits, slowly made our way past the Capitol, then the Cathedral, we drifted past the next three exits, and then Luscious followed Lissa's red BMW when it took the Snelling Avenue exit off the interstate. Dondavitch relayed the information to me, bringing up the rear.

"Thank God, we're taking the Snelling exit. God, following at that speed we were going so slow it was damn near illegal. People were starting to give us the damn finger."

"If she heads north on Snelling, she more than likely is heading to her place."

"North it is," Dondavitch said a minute later. "We got her address up here on the screen."

"You might want to alert a unit in the area."

"Gee, thanks for the advice, how did we ever make it this far without you? We've already done that."

Forty-six

A few miles later, we all took a right off Snelling onto Arlington. A small parade of four vehicles, with Lissa's BMW in the lead and Luscious governing the pace in the rental pickup just behind her. Dondavitch held back a good block behind them. As I made the turn off Snelling, I caught the tail end of Lissa's BMW before it turned into an alley. Luscious followed behind her in the pickup. I pulled to the curb two blocks behind Dondavitch.

"Haskell," Dondavitch half screamed into the phone. I could see her car pulled over with the brake lights on. I couldn't tell the make, some nondescript Ford or Chevy I figured. It looked like she was almost at the entrance to the alley Lissa, and Luscious had driven down just a moment before.

"Yeah?"

"We've got a squad ready to come down at the far end of the alley. Let's give your gal a few minutes. When I give you the go-ahead, I want you to knock on the front door. That will probably send them out the back."

"Did you tell that other squad about Luscious, that he'll be in there, and he's one of us?"

"Yes, they have a description, I suspect he'll be rather hard to miss."

"Just so they know."

"They know."

A few minutes later, Dondavitch said, "Okay, we're ready. Here's what I want, Haskell. You just knock on the front door. Don't go in. We'll be coming around the back. The uniforms will pound on the back door."

"It's on the north side of the house, the back door."

"Thanks, the two of us will come around the side and join you at the front. Give us half a minute to get in position before you go. You aware of any dogs, any locked gates?"

"No dogs, as far as I know. There's a fence around the back yard, but I think there's a gate on all sides, no locks that I can remember."

"Then we're all set, and let's go, thirty seconds, Haskell. Remember give us thirty seconds."

I saw the brake lights go off on her vehicle, she quickly turned into the alley and disappeared from view. I drove down toward Lissa's street, slowly counting. When I reached twenty, I turned onto the street and headed for her house. I was able to pull to the curb right in front of her place.

The house was a two-story stucco structure dating from probably the late 1930s. It had a small front porch with a roof, and then next to that, running along the front was a wooden deck with a railing, a nice bench, and two pots with pink geraniums.

As I climbed out of my car, I caught sight of Dondavitch and another woman just making their way around the back corner of the house. A moment later, I heard heavy pounding from the other side of the house as a deep voice bellowed, "Police. Open up," then the pounding started again.

I took the four front steps two at a time and was about to knock on the door just as it tore open. Lissa was in the process of rushing out with Candi right behind her. I heard a large groan from inside, and my first thought was they'd done something to Luscious.

"What the…Oh no, Dev, hey, sorry, but this really isn't a very good time for us, so just get the hell out of the way."

More pounding from the back and another, "Police. Open the door."

"Get your ass back inside, both of you," I said, just as Dondavitch and her partner came up with guns drawn and badges hanging from around their neck.

"Back off, Haskell, we got this," Dondavitch said as she and her partner brushed past me.

I followed them into a carpeted living room. There was a couch with a small table at one end and a flatscreen at the other end. Andy's hand-carved, black walnut coffin sat on the floor in front of the couch with a deck of cards, an ashtray and a dish full of M&Ms sitting on top of it.

Luscious was in the archway leading to the dining room, he was down on the floor, or rather Tommy Flaherty was on the floor groaning and attempting to squirm with Luscious sitting on top of him. Luscious was eating a handful of M&Ms, one at a time. At first, I thought Tommy was having a seizure then I realized the red face and hands were probably due to the dye pack from the ATM. We were all just standing there, staring as Luscious smiled back at us.

A loud boom suddenly sounded from the back of the house as the door was kicked in, and the two uniforms came through the kitchen and into the dining room with guns drawn shouting, "Police."

"Just what in the hell do you think you're doing, Dev?" Lissa snarled, then placed her hands on her hips, and struck a don't screw with me pose.

Dondavitch answered for me and said, "Put your hands on your head and get down on your knees, both of you, now, move."

"But, I didn't do anything," Candi cried.

"Move, bitch, now."

I couldn't have said it any better. One of the uniforms was helping Luscious to his feet while the other had rolled Tommy onto his stomach and was busy slapping on a set of handcuffs. Tommy just looked grateful to be sucking in huge gulps of air.

"Yeah, I already know, I got the right to remain silent. Shit, nice work, Lissa, way to check things out," Tommy groaned.

"Me, more like that pimp pal of yours, Tony," Lissa shot back.

"Shut up, bitch."

"Maybe all of you should just shut up," Dondavitch said.

Luscious made his way into the living room and grabbed the bowl of M&Ms off the coffin. I strolled into the dining room where two more coffins were stacked one on top of the other in front of a china cabinet full of plates and little figurines. I opened the top coffin. It was half-filled with cash, a lot of which was stained red.

I wandered into the small kitchen then peeked down the dark basement stairs. I flicked on the light switch for the stairway and headed down. A few miles of clothesline was strung back and forth numerous times across the paneled basement room. Hundreds, no make that thousands, of red, twenty-dollar bills were paper clipped to the line and seemed to be blowing in a breeze. A couple of oscillating fans turned back and forth, at either end of the basement.

I walked into the room where the washer and dryer stood. Two piles of clothes were neatly folded and stacked on a table against the wall. Next to the washer was a double laundry tub. It looked original to the house, deep, made of concrete, and sitting on a steel frame. Both sides of the laundry tub were filled with pinkish water and looked to be crammed with more red, twenty dollar bills floating in the water, signifying yet another failed attempt at criminal enterprise by Tommy Flaherty.

I unhooked a couple of the bills from the clothesline and went back upstairs to the living room. The three Flahertys were seated with their hands cuffed behind their backs. Tommy was on the floor red-faced, and looking numb. Lissa and Candi sat at opposite ends of the couch, staring straight ahead. Lissa looked ready to kill, and Candi softly whimpered as tears ran down her cheeks.

"Really nice to see you again, Candi. I suppose with those handcuffs on, there's really no way you could show me what I was missing the other night."

"Hope you're happy, asshole," Lissa shouted at me from the other end of the couch.

"Very," I replied and smiled.

"Transport's on the way," Dondavitch said.

"Little something for you, from the basement," I said and handed her the damp, red twenties.

"Apparently, there's a hearse parked out in the garage. Where'd you find these?" she asked holding one of the red bills up toward the window light.

"Basement is full of them."

"You're violating my damn rights, Haskell, I demand to talk to a lawyer," Lissa shouted from the couch.

"You haven't even been arrested, let alone charged yet, honey. Just settle down for a bit, you're gonna have plenty of time to think about what you'll say," Dondavitch said.

Forty-seven

It was well past noon by the time Luscious, and I finished giving our statements to the police. The bowl of M&Ms had been emptied, twice, and the empty bag lay crumpled on Lissa's dining room table. I found Luscious in the kitchen, standing in front of the open refrigerator door scanning the contents for anything edible and not looking too happy.

"Luscious, what are you doing?"

"All this excitement going on, I'm about to faint from hunger, Dev. Nothing but a jar of pickles and some kind of pasta sauce in here. That stuff don't exactly thrill me."

"Hey, there's a McDonald's about a mile and a half from here. My treat if you're interested."

That brought a smile to his face, and he stood up, kicked the refrigerator door closed, and said, "Now you're talking, you just lead the way."

We said our good-byes to Detective Dondavitch. Red-dyed Tommy Flaherty was already on his way to the police station. Two detectives were in the basement, gathering trash bags full of evidence. Tommy's two lovely sisters, Lissa and Candi, remained sitting on the couch, hands still cuffed behind their backs awaiting transport.

Candi sat there quietly sobbing with puffy eyes and mascara running down her cheeks. Lissa still hadn't lost any of the anger from two hours earlier and in fact, appeared to be even more enraged. She sneered at me as I walked from the dining room over to the couch. Luscious followed behind, stopping to double-check the crumpled M&M bag for crumbs.

"Gee, sorry to dash off like this, girls, but I'm afraid we've got another appointment. Otherwise I'd stay and chat."

"Can't you do something? I'm really sorry, but we didn't know," Candi sobbed.

"I'll kill you, Dev. I swear to God, I'm going to kill you," Lissa hissed.

"Detective, did you hear that, a death threat. Can she do that? Isn't there some law against that sort of thing?"

"I think we'll be able to add that to her list of charges," Dondavitch said. Then she took out a pen and wrote something down in a pocket-size spiral notebook. When she'd finished, she held the notebook up so I could read what she'd written. "Very angry bitch." She'd drawn a smiley face image, but with a frown just after that.

"Yes, that will be perfect. Gee, I guess I'll just have to say farewell, girls. It's been a real pleasure. Payback can be such fun. You'll probably be old and grey by the time you get out. If you ever do get out. Enjoy the vacation," I said.

"Old and grey?" Candi whined, looked over at her sister, and then began to sob uncontrollably.

"Shut up, Candi, he doesn't know what the hell he's talking about, and by the way, you were the worst lay I ever had, Dev. You hear me, the worst, ever. Ev-er," Lissa screamed from the couch as we stepped outside.

"You know her, personally, like?" Dondavitch asked out on the front porch.

"Yeah, both of them, from years back, but I didn't know they were involved in this thing until Lissa showed up at Denny's this morning. What do you think they'll get?" I asked.

"The brother will probably get up to twenty years. He's got a list of priors as long as your arm. The girls, unless I missed something, it's a first for both of them. Probably five years probation, pee in a paper cup for sixty months and promise to behave. Even if they were involved in the ATM heist, they can dodge that without too much trouble, well, unless the brother turns, but that's not going to happen."

"What a bunch of idiots. Must be something in the gene pool."

"That's a pretty strong indictment coming from the likes of you, Haskell," she said and smiled.

Luscious had pulled the pickup truck around the block, and I could see him coming down the street.

"Glad I could be of help, how long will you hang onto those coffins."

"God, what a creepy deal that is. Maybe they'll make 'World's Dumbest Criminals.' How long? Depends on when they're brought to trial. They all plead guilty that speeds things up. Be at least a couple of months. Is there a rush?"

"No, I guess not."

Luscious honked the horn on the pickup and motioned me toward the street.

"Looks like my crime-fighting partner is getting anxious, I better go."

"Thanks again, I mean it. Things were getting cold on the ATM, so we all appreciate the help."

Luscious honked the horn again.

"Better hurry, he's no doubt wasting away," Dondavitch said.

"We're about to take care of that. If you could find it in your heart to keep the ladies locked up for an extended time in maybe your grimiest cell, it would be okay with me," I said then hurried to my car before Luscious died of hunger.

Forty-eight

I retrieved the envelope with cash from Luscious. I'd learned from past experience that it would work best if we went inside to eat rather than attempting to cram a couple hundred pounds of Big Macs and fries into the car.

Luscious was easily the size of any four individuals in the place, and he hurried to a booth in the back carrying two trays mounded with food and three strawberry shakes. He inhaled a double cheeseburger along the way just to keep his strength up. I carried the tray with all the desserts plus my cheeseburger and small coke. More than a few heads turned as we passed, then they would lean forward to whisper to one another once they realized it was just the two of us and all that food. I noticed the young woman who took our order leaning over the counter to watch as Luscious waddled toward the rear booth.

By the time I sat down, Luscious was cramming half of a Big Mac into his mouth and reaching for one of the strawberry shakes. I knew better than to get between him and food, and there was certainly no point in attempting conversation. So, we sat there in relative silence while I finished my cheeseburger. Then I stretched out on my side of the booth, sipped my Coke, and people watched. After thirty minutes, Luscious had cleared off two entire trays and was beginning to work his way through the desserts, washing them down with a strawberry shake.

"How is it, good?" I asked.

A man focused on the mission at hand. He simply nodded and continued eating. At about the fifty-minute mark, he pushed the final, empty tray off to the side, tilted his head back, closed his eyes, and let out a very loud and long belch. The air suddenly smelled of strawberry shake and French fries. The couple across the aisle from us immediately got up and walked swiftly out the door.

"Luscious, you still have that final strawberry shake left. Hope you're not going to let that go to waste."

"No, sir, I'm saving that for the drive back to that rental place."

It served me right for asking, and I didn't dare ask if he wanted anything else. "You ready to head out?"

"I think it's time," he said like we had both been waiting for me to finish some task, then he cupped the shake in a massive paw and groaned as he got to his feet. Our table was awash in wrappers, and just about every head in the place watched us as we walked toward the door.

"Good-bye, thanks for choosing McDonald's," the woman who had waited on us called, as Luscious oozed out the side door.

"You follow me, okay, Luscious? I'm going to pull onto that street behind the rental place, and we'll switch drivers again, so it looks like I drove the truck this afternoon, got it?"

Luscious sucked down about an inch of strawberry shake and nodded, then climbed behind the wheel of the pickup. The thing leaned far enough to the left that it looked like the shocks were broken on that side.

It's not a busy street running past McDonald's, but we had to wait for a couple of cars to pass, we made a right out of the parking lot and then about fifty feet down the road I made a sharp left. Unfortunately, Luscious did not. Focused on his strawberry shake, he missed the turn, then to make matters worse, he apparently mistook the accelerator for the brake pedal and floored the pickup about fifteen feet before hitting a tree.

The hood buckled, the front bumper was dented, and the grill was hanging in two pieces. If I had to guess, I'd say there was about three to four grand worth of damage to the truck. Luscious stepped out with a guilty look on his face, at least I thought he looked guilty. It was hard to tell with strawberry shake dripping down his chin.

"What the hell happened?"

"I think a strawberry got stuck in my straw."

"A what? Luscious, there aren't any strawberries in those shakes, it just strawberry flavored. Didn't you see the tree?" Which I knew was a stupid question before I finished asking it. I remembered the guy at the rental place saying, *'You want our rider insurance? Forty-five bucks, don't mind me saying it might not be a bad idea.'*

It took the better part of an hour to fill out the accident report at the rental place. We'd called the police on the way over, but they're stretched so thin in our town that unless there's someone injured, they don't have the manpower to dispatch someone. They took my name and address and said they'd mail out an accident form for insurance purposes then gave me a website address if I wanted to download the form myself.

The two guys at the rental place were still sipping coffee and acted like they weren't all that surprised. "But you were driving, is that correct, Mr. Haskell?" It was the fourth time they'd asked me.

"Yeah, I told you before, it was either the tree or hit some senior citizen on a motorized wheelchair. I didn't have any choice, isn't that right, Luscious?"

"Just like he said," Luscious replied, not taking his eyes off his feet.

The rental guy looked at the two of us for a long moment then decided there wasn't anything he could do to improve the situation. "Okay, we'll be in touch. Have a nice day," he said, flashed a smile for a nanosecond, and sent us on our way.

I took the scenic route along the river as I drove Luscious home then stopped in front of the steps to his building. "Luscious, it's been real, thanks again for your help. I'll have a check in the mail to you tomorrow if that's okay." I was turned partially around, talking to him stretched out in the back seat.

"Be fine with me, Mr. Dev. Real sorry bout that little bump and spilling that shake and all," he said, sounding genuinely apologetic.

"Not a problem, based on what we did today, I'd say we got off easy."

That brought a smile to his face, and then my car rocked back and forth as he climbed out of the back seat. "Be seeing you now. You need my help again you just call me, Mr. Dev." Then he stood on the curb and waved as I drove off.

Forty-nine

My phone rang as I was pulling into my driveway.

"Haskell Investigations."

"I hear congratulations are in order." It was Aaron LaZelle.

"Yeah, things worked out pretty well for a change. I recovered those coffins, and my hunch paid off for Dondavitch,"

"Apparently, there were some unhappy campers on the scene."

"You mean the sisters?"

"Yeah."

"Well, hopefully, this will shake them up, and they'll fly right. The good detective seemed to think they'll get off with probation. Their brother probably won't be quite so lucky."

"It always amazes me how many times people get caught, and they still think they can get away with shit. That kid will be north of forty years old before he sees the light of day."

"Yeah, the sad thing is he's actually a pretty nice guy if he would just get his act together, but he just never seems to do that."

"Some guys never do. Anyway, I just wanted to say thanks. You still owe me dinner, by the way."

"Just let me know when you're free."

"You're safe for the foreseeable future."

I'd barely hung up when my phone rang again.

"Hello, Dev? It's Gemma, can you talk?"

I was parked in my driveway. "Yeah, Gemma, go ahead."

"Royal has another board meeting tonight. It's at the Venture Inn out on 694."

"He told you where it's at? Doesn't that suggest it might be legit?"

"Actually, he didn't tell me. I've gotten in the habit of checking the calendar on his home computer. It's linked to the business. He's nothing if not thorough. He even had the confirmation number and the name of the hotel listed for tonight."

"Did you get his 'I'm going to be late' call yet?"

"No, those usually don't come through for another couple of hours. But I thought I'd give you a call, maybe give you a little more time."

I was writing down the hotel name, I knew approximately where it was, but I'd never been in the place. "Can you print off that calendar without his knowledge?"

"I can do just about anything I want without Royal's knowledge," she said and left that statement hanging out there for a moment. "Besides, I was a pretty good programmer at one time in my life."

"One more unfortunate piece of the puzzle, if you could go back and print off his calendar for say the past six months to a year, it wouldn't necessarily be *the* smoking gun, but it would help to build your case."

"Actually, I've already done that, and for exactly that reason. I went through the last year, and I have to say I've been pretty stupid. Real stupid as a matter of fact. God, I could just scream."

Gemma was beginning to make me think she wasn't quite the helpless soul I'd first thought.

Fifty

The Venture Inn looks just like what it is, an eight-story brick hotel set on the edge of a busy freeway with fairly convenient access to the airport and both downtowns. A half dozen chain restaurants and three gas stations were within sight of the entrance to the place.

I was in the parking lot, two rows back from the front door when Royal finally showed up. I'd been sitting in my car for almost an hour. I took a couple of pictures of him getting out of his car and walking inside. His luggage consisted of what looked like two bottles of Champagne.

Ashley and dunderhead Tony arrived almost an hour after Royal. She was dressed in an appropriately hot looking skirt with a different sequined belt, a top that appeared to be open almost down to her navel and the same knee-high black boots with stiletto heels. Tony was in jeans and a t-shirt that looked like they should have been thrown in the wash early last week.

I waited about five minutes, then entered the hotel. The bar was just across the lobby from the front desk. I could see Tony in there nursing a beer and already filling a plastic basket with losing pull tabs, fortunately, his back was to me.

I approached the front desk with a smiling guy standing behind it. He looked to be about mid-forties with slightly graying temples and brown frame glasses. He wore a starched blue shirt with a navy blue blazer and a conservative tie, apparently the uniform for front desk staff.

"Hi, welcome to the Venture Inn, how can I help you?"

"I'm supposed to meet up with a business associate here. Can you direct me to his room? Royal Baker is his name."

"Let me get that information for you," he said and clicked half-a-dozen keys on the laptop in front of him. I figured I'd knock on the door then maybe grab a photo of Royal and Ashley, hopefully, while she was just wearing a smile.

"Sure, here it is, you can reach him on this extension," he said then wrote the extension number down on a hotel business card. It was the same drill I'd received the last time I was tracking Royal on one of his trysts, and I guessed it was a standard hotel routine. I smiled and took the card.

"There's a house phone right over there," he nodded to a counter attached to the wall on the far side of the lobby. The phone was next to a little stand filled with a variety of tourist brochures. I was about to say thanks when a voice behind me yelled out. "Haskell?"

I turned to see Tony coming out of the bar. He had a wide-eyed look on his face as he stopped and just stood there staring at me.

I wasn't sure which of us was more surprised and decided to play the part. "Tony? What are you doing here?"

I thought I might have caught him off guard because he stuttered. "Oh, yeah, I got a call, and I was just driving past and thought this looked like a nice joint, so I decided to go in and grab a beer."

God, he wasn't even a good liar. I noticed the fingertips on both his hands were still red, just like Tommy Flaherty's face and hands had been. Unfortunately, he'd apparently recovered enough not to have his arm still in the sling.

"How's Ashley doing? Is she *working* tonight?" I asked and raised my eyebrows.

"Ash? Oh, no, not here tonight. But, she's doing pretty well, you know with work and everything. Course all those online problems she was having, I think I got that nailed down."

"You ever find out who that was?"

"Hey, Haskell, if you're lookin' to scam more business, you can just forget it. Like I said, I already did my own investigation, and I got a pretty good idea. Went back and reviewed some things, checked out those images that had been posted, the dates they were posted. Once I did that, the pattern became pretty obvious, and it didn't cost an arm and a leg, either."

"Oh good, so you know who did it?"

"Like I said, I got a pretty good idea."

In other words, he didn't have a clue.

"That's good, Tony, real good. How about you let me buy you a beer? You can tell me all about your investigative technique, how you did it, and we can celebrate the fact that you don't need your arm in a sling anymore. You know, from when that little guy kicked your ass the other day."

"Actually, much as I'd like to have you buy, I gotta meet someone in the lobby here in a while."

"Ashley?"

"No, she ain't here, it's someone else, they're delivering a package."

"Delivering a package? To you? I thought you said you just ducked in for a beer?"

"Yeah, I did, but then Royal sent me a text message, said to run interference and get this package. You know, since I'm already here, they can run it over to me."

"Then you'll run it up to Royal's room?"

"Yeah, he wants to get it right— no not up to Royal's room. I told you, he ain't even here. I don't know where the hell he is, home, or somewhere. I'm gonna deliver it to him later tonight, probably at his house, that is once I get the thing."

"Too bad he's not here, it would save you some time."

"I don't mind. I better get going, that delivery probably will be here any minute, then I'll be taking off," he said, and took a few steps in the direction of the men's room.

"Always a pleasure, Tony."

He nodded, suggesting the opportunity to talk with him was just that, a pleasure.

Fifty-one

Tony's bullshit about having a package delivered to him was laughable and suggested a host of other issues. If I had to guess, I'd say he was a lot more uncomfortable with Ashley's line of work than he was letting on, especially if one of her top customers was the same guy who was making it all possible. I retreated back to the sanity of the front seat of my car, turned on the radio and waited for Royal and Ashley to reappear in the hope I might get to photograph a goodbye kiss or some other, equally stupid move.

It was maybe an hour later when I saw an older woman entering the hotel lobby carrying what looked like a white bakery box. Her hair was a nondescript brown and cut in a short bob. She wore expensive casual clothes. Maybe twenty minutes after that, I was in the midst of switching radio stations again when it happened; there was a rumble, but too loud to be a car, and it seemed to come from above. As I looked up, I saw the windows of a room blowing off the side of the building four or five floors up and disintegrating in mid-air.

Almost immediately, there was the sound of a bell ringing, like an alarm bell, although not too loud. As I climbed out of my car, bits and pieces of debris and dust were drifting down to the ground. I just stood there staring up at the hole in the side of the building. The parking lot began filling up with crazed guests and hotel staff rushing out of the front door.

Some guy in jeans and a t-shirt, was directing people further and further away from the building, and no one seemed to be in the frame of mind to give him an argument. As people hurried across the parking lot, what was left of the drapes fluttered out the charred remains of the window, and a set of Venetian blinds hung by a long cord and dangled down to the floor below.

More and more people exited the building, some came to stand below the hole in the side of the building and just stare upwards, but the majority of people moved away from the building and stood behind me on the far side of the parking lot. Guys in business suits, what looked like kitchen staff in white coats and checkered pants, a couple of waitresses wearing aprons, the guy from behind the front desk, and some kids in swim suits all lined up on the edge of the parking lot.

After a few minutes, you could hear the sound of sirens growing closer, and just moments later, first one and then two fire trucks raced in and parked in front of the main entry, with their lights flashing. Two more rigs arrived after that, firemen in helmets and heavy equipment climbed off the vehicles and moved inside the building, not wasting any time.

Two squad cars arrived at about the same time. The officers began to move everyone out of the parking lot, myself included. I ended up standing next to three little boys in swimsuits with their mom holding an empty wine glass. I scanned the crowd back and forth looking for Tony, Ashley, and Royal, but couldn't see them.

Another fire truck arrived along with the paramedics. A couple of people were in the crowd with their luggage. First one and then two more news vehicles arrived, but the police wouldn't let them into the parking lot. None of us were allowed to go to our cars, so all we could do was just stand there and watch, not that there was anything left to see.

A couple of firemen appeared briefly in the room where the explosion had occurred and gazed out of the charred hole in the wall. I don't know if they were looking to see if someone was hanging onto the side of the building or if they just wanted to see how high up they were. Behind them, you could see what looked like the remains of a table lamp and a framed painting or print hanging sideways on the wall.

It was much later that night before they began letting people back into the building, and then only registered guests to get their luggage. People were streaming out of the building, rolling suitcases behind them, and heading for their cars. The police were checking everyone off a list before they were allowed to drive away, presumably to look for another place to stay. I had to wait another hour and a half before I was able to get in my car and drive home.

I drove back past the place the following morning. There were still maybe a dozen cars in the hotel lot. Four or five of the cars were parked just below the site of the explosion and appeared to be too damaged from falling debris to be driven. There were a couple of squad cars and two fire department vehicles near the front door and then off to the side and well away from the blast area. Royal's car was parked exactly where I'd seen him pull in last night. About thirty yards from Royal's car, Tony's car sat looking abandoned in the all but empty parking lot. I slowed but didn't stop and headed to my office.

Vague information was on the radio news, but nothing that I didn't already know. There had been a "fire" at the Venture Inn, and the place had been evacuated, the cause was unknown at this time. Nothing much after that, I got into the office a little after nine, Louie was nowhere to be seen. I phoned Gemma and ended up leaving a message asking her to call me when she had a moment.

She phoned me maybe a half-hour later.

"Dev, this is Gemma." She sounded, I don't know, distracted maybe.

"Gemma, thanks for returning my call. I was at the Venture Inn last night, I don't know if you saw it on the news, but there was…."

"The police left maybe an hour ago. I wasn't feeling well and took a sleeping pill last night, didn't wake up until they were pounding on the door this morning. I figured Royal had already left for work."

I waited for her to say something else, but she didn't.

"Is he at the office?" I finally asked.

"No, apparently there was an explosion or fire or something, and, well, he won't be coming home."

"Is he okay?"

"No, they think he might be dead. He had a room there, at the Venture Inn, it's where the explosion happened."

"Are you okay, Gemma?"

"What? I don't know. I'm just trying to get my head around this whole thing. I really don't know what to think."

I didn't think she sounded that upset, considering the police had just told her that Royal was most likely blown to bits just last night in a hotel explosion. "Is there anything I can do for you?"

"No, no, I think I just need some time. My mother's on her way over now. I'll be okay, I think."

Fifty-two

I thought about my brief phone conversation with Gemma for the rest of the morning. I called Aaron LaZelle just after my late lunch and left a message. He phoned me back toward the end of the day. I was in The Spot, sitting at the bar talking to Louie.

"Yeah, Dev, you called." He said it in that clipped way he has when he's juggling a half dozen different things, suggesting I had better make it fast.

"Thanks for returning my call, Aaron. That Venture Inn explosion…."

"I really don't know much more than what you hear on the news right now. Not that I'd tell you, anyway. You need anything else?"

"Actually, the reason I'm calling is I was there."

"What do you mean, you were there?"

"I was there, in the parking lot, working. I saw the explosion and saw all the folks running out the door. I drove past this morning, and it turns out the guy I was investigating, doing surveillance on, his car was still in the lot along with another guy whose wife or girlfriend was meeting with the first guy and—"

"Just what in the hell are you talking about?"

"I was there trying to watch a guy named Royal Baker. He was supposedly having an affair with a woman named Ashley. She's some professional escort. I believe they were in the room together, her and Royal Baker. I met this jackass guy who drives this Ashley chick around, guy's name is Tony, don't know his last name. I ran into him in the hotel lobby, and he said he was waiting for a package to be delivered. Then he was going to take it to Baker. I don't know, maybe an hour later that explosion happened. I didn't put it together until this morning when I drove past, and the parking lot is basically empty except for their two cars."

"Any chance he might be somewhere else?"

"Who, Royal Baker? If he is, then you guys got a lot of explaining to do because his wife told me two officers had been there this morning giving her the bad news."

"I'm thinking you should probably come in so we can get a statement."

"When do you want me?"

"The sooner, the better."

"I'll be down there within the hour."

"I'm going to be meeting with the fire inspectors on their preliminary findings. When you get here ask for Manning."

"Manning? Oh come on, isn't there someone else that could do this?"

"Let me explain something, Dev. I just might have a few more irons in the fire than your inability to get on with Manning. No one else seems to have a problem, except for the bad guys. Get over it and then get your ass down here, pronto."

"What about tomorrow, would you have time then?"

"Dev. Hello? Are you listening? Did you hear anything I just said? I'll tell Manning you'll be down here within the hour, and I'll ask him to be gentle."

"I don't think he has it in him."

"One hour," Aaron said and hung up.

Fifty-three

I didn't know if Aaron's "hour" included the fifty-five minutes I had to wait locked in an interview room while Detective Norris Manning finished up whatever phone call he pretended to be on when I arrived. It was approaching the two-hour mark since I'd spoken with Aaron before Manning decided to make his appearance in the interview room.

He opened the door carrying a couple of files and a coffee mug. He marched over to the metal-topped table where I was sitting, cracking his ever-present wad of gum in time to his footsteps.

"So, Mr. Haskell, we meet once again. How are you? Well, I hope."

"Hey, look, Manning, I don't want to talk to you anymore than you want to talk to me. So, let's just get this statement over with, and then I can go home, and you can hassle some other innocent citizen."

"Amazingly, there seems to be multiple homicides in our saintly city, and you just happen to be in the area. Imagine my surprise." He smiled, but his cold blue eyes bored in on me like lasers. The pink dome of his bald head flushed ever so slightly as he opened the file in

Double Trouble ◆ 259

front of him. "Why don't you start at the beginning and enlighten me."

"Okay, I was hired by a Mrs. Gemma Baker to investigate her suspicions concerning her husband, Royal Baker, and his possibly being involved in an extramarital affair."

"How did she hear about you?" he asked and turned a page in the file.

"I was working for her husband, well, at least until we parted ways."

Manning looked up. "He fired you?"

"It was more of a mutual decision. He had me looking into some online harassment of one of his clients, and I didn't get along with the client or her companion, for that matter."

"There's a surprise. So Baker terminated the contract?"

"Yes."

"And his wife hired you?"

"Yes"

"Was she involved in any way with the earlier arrangement between you and Mr. Baker?"

"No, not to my knowledge. As far as I know, she's not involved in his business."

"And what did she want you to do?"

"She told me she was going to initiate divorce proceedings against her husband, Royal Baker. She suspected him of having an ongoing sexual relationship with one of his clients, a woman named Ashley. I was to obtain proof of that relationship."

"And how did you intend to do that, obtain proof?"

"About all I had were some photographs, the usual things, their cars in hotel parking lots, the two of them entering and leaving the hotel."

"Did they actually do this, arrive or leave in one another's company? Walk arm in arm, or something?"

"No, that was part of the problem. Baker would arrive maybe close to an hour before her. She'd leave before he did. She was always with some guy named Tony, no last name. A real jerk, anyway, this Tony would drive her to the hotel then wait in the bar while she was riding Baker for a couple of hours up in some room, and then they'd leave together."

"This Ashley and Tony person?"

"Yeah."

"So, although you had strong suspicions you never found anything incriminating."

"Yeah, that's pretty accurate."

"And you get paid for this?"

"You know, Manning, I'm down here on my own time trying to help you through an investigation. Could we just get on with it, I'm not the one under investigation, here."

"Yet," he smiled then said, "Okay, strike that last comment about getting paid. Nothing should surprise me anymore. So what were you doing, just hanging around the bar?"

"No, I was out in the parking lot, sitting in my car. I went into the hotel to see if I could get Baker's room number, I couldn't. Instead, they gave me a phone extension to call his room. Before I could do anything, this Tony character spotted me, and we talked for just a minute."

"What did he say?"

"Nothing worthwhile, except that he denied Baker and Ashley were at the hotel. But, I'd seen both of them entering earlier that evening. Then he told me he was waiting for a package to arrive, and he was supposed to deliver it to Baker, at his home."

"Arrive? You mean in the mail?"

I looked at Manning for a long moment. "No, somebody was dropping the thing off to him at the hotel. Then he was supposed to give the thing to Baker."

"At Baker's house?"

"Yeah, at least that's what he said. I think he was trying to blow smoke, you know, convince me Baker and that Ashley chick weren't there. I had the feeling he knew it wasn't working, and that I was on to them."

"He tell you who this package was supposed to be from?"

"Nope."

"Do you know if he ever received this package?"

I shook my head. "No. I did see a woman carrying a bakery box, you know those white things, but I don't know if it was the package that this Tony guy was waiting for. I never saw the woman leave the hotel, and I was watching the front door, well, up until that explosion."

"I'm sure *you* wouldn't miss anything," Manning half mumbled.

"So, who else was killed besides Royal Baker?" I asked.

Manning looked up from his file and studied me for a moment. "We have two other bodies, an adult male and female. We're confirming identification right now. Then we'll notify next of kin. It will probably be on the ten o'clock news. You could watch the broadcast from whatever bar you're in."

"Sounds like it could be this Ashley and Tony, although given the nature of the business she had with Baker that may not be her real name. I think he might have the records at his business, Tri-Cort Services, they're out just off of I-94, a couple of blocks from…."

"Someone's out there checking that now."

"Well, while they're checking, the other male body, the guy I knew as Tony, see if he had any relation to Tommy Flaherty, the guy that got nailed on those ATM heists. I noticed what looked like red dye on his fingertips. It looked like the stuff Flaherty was covered with when he was arrested. One of Flaherty's sisters made a remark about his pimp friend, Tony. Could be they were connected."

Manning seemed to ignore my suggestion and said, "Tell me about your initial hire, working for Baker."

Double Trouble ♦ 263

"Not much to tell, Baker hired me to find out who was posting images of this Ashley woman on her 'dating' web site."

"Images?"

"Not what you're probably thinking of, usually no sexual stuff, at least that I know of. It was just shots of her going in or coming out of a hotel, standing by a tree, or some other dumb thing most of the time. There was one, and it led to me quitting the investigation, where she and that Tony guy were doing it on the hood of his car in a parking ramp."

Manning made a quick face like that didn't make any sense. "For what purpose?"

"Purpose? Maybe they just felt like screwing. I don't know. None of it really made any sense, although this Ashley said her business was down ten or fifteen percent, I can't remember the figure. Based on her line of work, you'd think an image of her banging on the hood of a car might even be a good marketing campaign."

"Did you find out who was taking these images and posting them?"

I shook my head. "Baker, or actually, both of us terminated the contract before I had the chance. Not that I ever had any idea."

Manning frowned and nodded, suggesting that wasn't surprising.

"No one was really cooperating. I was just glad to be finished with the bunch of them."

"You weren't upset? I could see how you'd be upset. That sort of thing can really hurt a reputation."

"Save it, Manning. I wasn't upset, believe me, I was ready to quit anyway. It's not like I needed the hassle."

"Of course, plus with the state of your so-called reputation already, well. Any final thoughts?"

"You mean who might have done it?"

"Yes," he said, then bored into me with those laser eyes.

"No, to be specific. In general terms, it would have to be someone familiar with the locations. Someone with the time to do it. Someone with the time and inclination to follow either Baker or Ashley around. Well, and know how to, or know someone who would know how to build an explosive device."

"Sounds like you'd fit the bill," Manning said, then just stared at me without smiling.

Fifty-four

Manning chatted and made some more notes in his file, then finally looked up. "Okay, Mr. Haskell, I really don't have anything else for you at this time, and unfortunately, no current reason to hold you, maybe just plan on keeping yourself available should something come across the radar."

"I'll be sure to do that, Detective. I'm free to go?"

"I'm sure we'll be in touch, but please, by all means, get the hell out of my sight." And so I did.

Once I was finished wasting time with Manning, I headed over to Andy's place.

"God, I couldn't believe it when that Detective Dondavitch called," Andy groaned in his office. I had been sitting there listening for the past fifteen minutes to how well Tommy Flaherty had been working collections for him.

"Dondavitch was pretty good," I said. "They got Tommy Flaherty for stealing three different ATMs. I mean he stole the entire machine, I saw the tape of one of the heists. He and some other guy just tossed the thing into the back of a hearse and drove off with it. Course they apparently hadn't figured on this red dye exploding all over the place. One of your coffins had a bunch of cash stuffed in it. There was a few grand worth of twenty's hanging up to dry in the basement, still dyed red and worthless. Tommy looked like someone had attacked him with an ax with all the red dye still coating him. All three of your coffins were in his sister's house."

Andy just shook his head. "You gonna send me an invoice?"

"You know what? I'm not. I was the one who suggested Tommy Flaherty to you in the first place. Maybe we'll just call it even, and next time I recommend someone, you can just ignore me."

"Not your fault, I was the guy who interviewed and then hired that stupid son of a bitch."

"Yeah, but remember, I gave you his name."

"Too bad, he's actually got some real talent. I could have seen him working his way into other positions. He's certainly not stupid."

"Like one of my cop pals said, some folks just think they're too smart to get caught."

Andy's phone rang, "This is probably our insurance guy wondering why we can't put the deceased in the coffin with a family crest on it even though the guy's been buried for a week. I better take this."

I waved goodbye as he picked up the phone.

I phoned Heidi to see if she might be able to improve my mood after I'd been locked in a room with Manning.

"What?" she answered.

"Hey, I'm looking for a gorgeous woman who might be interested in dinner and maybe a glass or two of Prosecco."

"You're looking to get laid."

"Well, yeah, but we wouldn't have to do that on an empty stomach."

"Thanks, but no thanks. I'm going to a lecture tonight."

"A what?"

"Yeah, you heard right, a lecture. Its high class, so it's way out of your league, investments with a green future."

"What?"

"Climate change, Dev, global warming. It's been in all the papers. It's even mentioned on TV, you probably could have caught it at The Spot, if they ever bothered to turn the sound up on the TV."

"Maybe I should go with you, and then we could just grab something later on."

"I'm meeting someone there, so no. And anyway, I don't really feel like being grabbed."

"Since when?"

"Nice chatting, good-bye," she said and hung up.

I ran down a list of potential dates in my mind, but every name I came up with had vowed to hang up on me if they ever heard my voice again, so I headed down to The Spot.

Fifty-five

I'd been nursing a couple of beers and chatting with Jimmy off and on for the past couple of hours when the ten o'clock news came on.

"Jimmy, turn up the sound, I want to hear what they say about that hotel explosion."

"It'll bother the other customers, Dev."

I looked around. There was a couple who'd been arguing in a back booth for the past hour, a guy at the far end of the bar who just stared at his beer and hadn't uttered a word since he'd walked in the door and then there was me.

"Jimmy."

"Okay, okay," he said and picked up the remote.

The newscast led with a story about highway closures in the metro area, then they spent five minutes on the change to the starting times for junior high schools. Finally, just before the commercial break, they flashed three images on the screen; Royal Baker, Anthony Ceccio, and a woman named Joan Dillon. If you added a nose job, cheekbone enhancement, a few dozen Botox treatments, breast implants, and a new hair color Joan Dillon could be the woman I'd briefly known as Ashley.

It came as no surprise Anthony Ceccio's photo was actually a mug shot with a date, his name spelled out beneath the facial image and then "Lino Lakes" under that. He had apparently served time there just like Tommy Flaherty, and I was thinking possibly *with* Tommy. He still looked clueless. The forty-five-second news report closed with some outside footage of the hotel with a giant hole in the wall five stories up from the blasted out room, then they promised to cover the Twins latest loss right after the commercial break.

"There, happy?" Jimmy said and turned down the sound just as the lone guy seated at the far end got up and walked out the door. "Jesus, thanks, Dev. See, you're chasing away all my business."

"I don't think that guy even touched his beer. You can just serve it to the next poor soul that comes in."

Jimmy looked like he was considering that option.

"I should probably head home, too," I said and tossed a couple of bucks on the bar.

"You're gonna leave me with those two?" Jimmy said.

I turned to look at the couple in the back booth just as she drained her wine glass and gave the finger to the guy seated across from her. He slid out of the booth, grabbed her glass, and walked up to Jimmy.

"Another for my wife, I'll just have a coke," he said and slid the wine glass across the bar. Jimmy slid a coke back to him, then filled a relatively clean wine glass and slid it across.

"Keep the change," the guy said and tossed a ten on the bar.

"There you go, see, things are looking up," I said.

* * *

I got a phone call on my way into the office the following morning.

"Haskell Investigations."

"Mr. Haskell, please."

"Gemma?"

"Is this you, Dev?"

"Yeah, how are you doing?"

"I'm surviving, under the circumstances. You didn't happen to see the news last night, did you?"

"You mean the report about the explosion?"

"Yes, was that Joan Dillon person the woman he had been seeing?"

"I believe so, but I think there had been a lot of cosmetic work done between the time that photo was taken and the woman I met."

"It was her, I just know it. I've been in touch with the police, it's going to be another day or two, but as soon as they let me, I'm going over to Royal's office and review his files. I wonder if we might meet after that, by the way, I should be getting an invoice from you."

"I don't know what I'd charge you for, Gemma. Besides, given the way things turned out...."

"Nonsense, I won't hear of it. Send me an invoice, and I hope to talk with you later in the week, fair enough?"

"Very, I'll wait for your call."

"Thank you, we'll be in touch," she said and hung up.

Fifty-six

Gemma phoned three days later, and I set out to meet her at Royal Baker's office. Just like before, Marilynn came down to the lobby and escorted me up to the office. She looked a lot less formal, seemed a lot more relaxed, and even made a casual comment about the nice weather as we rode up to the executive suite.

"She's in her office, you can just go in," Marilynn said, then sat down at her desk and opened a Vogue magazine. I noticed there was a vase of fresh-cut flowers on a side table against the wall next to a plate of cookies. Her hair was styled in a shoulder-length way that actually looked rather nice.

Gemma was seated at Royal's desk, talking on the phone. She waved me in and pointed at one of the two chairs in front of the desk, then signaled she'd be finished in a moment.

"Dev, thanks for coming in, please tell me you brought that invoice," she said as she hung up the phone.

"I did, a little love letter," I said and handed her the envelope with my invoice.

"Thanks," she said, opened the envelope, then looked up at me. "This is it? Are you sure you're covered?"

"Yeah, it's just fine, really."

"Well, okay, let me just get a check cut for you, hang on," she said and got up from behind the desk.

As she walked out the door, I noticed the framed photo of her and Royal had been removed, in its place were two photos. One was just Gemma, smiling, sipping a glass of something on a veranda or balcony. A large body of water with a setting sun was behind her. The second image was she and Marilynn, at least I thought that's who it was. Her hair, Marilynn's, was different, short, bobbed, and I was thinking I'd seen her somewhere besides this office, but couldn't place it.

Gemma came back into the office with the plate of cookies. She sat down at the desk and handed a check to me. "Did you try one of these?" she said and pushed the cookies toward me.

"Oh, thanks, I better not."

"More the chocolate cake type?" she said and raised an eyebrow.

"Exactly."

She handed the check across the desk. "I hope this is all right, I told my mom to add a little bonus, I really appreciate your effort, Dev."

"Your mom?"

"Yeah, Marilynn, I'm sorry, I thought you knew. You mean Royal never mentioned it?"

"She's your mother? Marilynn? No, I had no idea. Is that her, there in that photo? The two of you. I didn't recognize her."

She glanced at the image. "Yeah, we were in Tuscany, two summers ago. Absolutely gorgeous. That's one of her casual wigs."

"Wigs?"

She leaned forward and almost whispered, "Androgenetic alopecia."

The blank look on my face must have spoken volumes.

"She suffers from hair loss, pretty severe thinning all over. She is so concerned about her appearance. I bet I haven't seen her without a wig the last ten or twelve years," she said, then glanced at the photo and smiled. "I'm really lucky. We've always been pretty close."

"So, is she going to help you close the business, maybe find a buyer?"

"What? Oh no, it will take me a while, but she'll help me to get up to speed. Remember, I'm a programmer, by way of training. Probably a little rusty, but mom will stay on until I'm able to fly solo. After all, this was where Royal and I met."

"You're going to take over and run the business?"

She smiled and nodded, but her eyes looked cold. It suddenly dawned on me where I thought I'd seen Marilynn, her mother. She'd been wearing that short bobbed wig, although I'd had no way of knowing it was a wig at the time. She was carrying a bakery box into the hotel just before the explosion that killed three people, one of whom was her boss and son-in-law, Royal.

"If there isn't anything else, I should probably get back to work. I've got a lot of catching up to do, years' worth," Gemma said as she stood.

"Yeah, let me get out of your way. Thank you, Gemma. Again, I'm sorry for your loss."

"Thank you, I guess we'll just have to move forward," she said, sounding like she already had.

"I guess so, thanks again. Please give me a call if I can be of any service."

Gemma nodded then sat back down. By the time I reached the door, she had begun clicking keys on her keyboard.

"Marilynn, it's been a pleasure. Thank you, can you escort me down?"

"Oh, you know the way, not to worry. Gemma's brought a breath of fresh air to the entire office."

"Yeah, I had no idea she was your daughter."

"Yes, she is," Marilynn said, then she gave me the exact same smile with the cold eye stare that Gemma had given just a moment earlier.

"I'll let myself out, thank you."

I was trying to think on the way to my car, but that wasn't working very well. Gemma and Marilynn, the woman with the bakery box, Ashley, Royal, that jerk Tony, it seemed to be adding up to Gemma maybe knowing a lot more than she had let on. I sat behind the wheel of my car for a good five minutes before I called Aaron. Surprisingly he answered.

"What?"

"Hey, I might have something on that explosion that killed Royal Baker and those two other people."

"Have something?"

I went on to explain the mother-daughter thing, the wig, the box, my suspicions.

"Wrong, as usual."

"What?"

"We went through the hotel security tapes. We've got the escort's husband taking the elevator up to the room with what looks like a cake box. That fits with the forensic analysis the BCA has, at least the preliminary results."

"A cake box, you mean one of those white things from a bakery, right?"

"Yeah, brought it up to the room where your pal Royal was hosting that escort, the other guy's wife."

"Ashley."

"That seems to have just been her stage name. Off stage, she was Joan Dillon."

"So they were married, I thought he was maybe just pimping her."

"He was pimping her. She just happened to be his wife, too. We've got indications she was going to leave him. She had a nest egg built up that he probably didn't know about. It looks like he was gonna leave the box there, get the hell out before they opened it. Unfortunately, they had probably already worked up an appetite, and they opened the box, ruined his day, along with theirs and that's pretty much it."

"What about Gemma Baker?"

"You mean your other client? I'm not sure what you're basing that on. We can't seem to find anything."

"There was apparently a computer in the Baker home that had access to Royal's calendar and other aspects of the business. Its how she knew they were getting together at the Venture Inn."

"They had a home computer like just about every other home in the western world. We checked, nothing like a calendar on it, no access to the business that we could find, we went over it pretty thoroughly."

"She's a programmer, and she happens to have some egghead degree in chemistry she could have deleted the business stuff and built a bomb, maybe…."

"Along with a million other folks, meanwhile Anthony 'Tony' Ceccio did time on a federal weapons charge a few years back. Not a big leap to place him in touch with someone who could build a device like the one that took out that hotel room. And, not a huge leap to have him stupid enough to still be in the room when the bomb detonated."

"But, I think it was Gemma Baker's mother who delivered that box to the hotel."

"Her mother? Is this the same woman who was Baker's second in command? She's gonna kill her son-in-law so her daughter can what, go back to work?"

"What about insurance money?"

"Yeah sure, but then why file for divorce? She stood to make more money getting a divorce settlement over the next twenty or thirty years with no risk of arrest. So why plant a bomb? It doesn't seem to make any sense."

"What if she was so pissed off with his ongoing affair she just wanted to get even?"

"Any proof? Any witness? God forbid, anything like evidence?"

"Well, no, not exactly."

"Yeah, that's why we're going with this Tony dunce with the federal weapons rap. You get something concrete, give me a call. But, the sense around here is we got this dead to rights, no pun intended, so if you call, it had better be good."

Fifty-seven

I was stretched out on the couch and on my third Mankato Ale. The twins were down by four runs, and it was only the top of the sixth. In between watching failed opportunities on my flatscreen, I was obsessing about Gemma's mom Marilynn delivering a bomb to Tony, who then promptly ran it up to Royal's room. The way I had it figured Tony was probably the one stupid enough to open the box and take all three of them out.

I slowly came awake at the sound of the doorbell. I took my time as I slipped my shoes on and made it out to the front door. I just barely caught a pair of taillights racing away from the curb and heading up the street. Not to worry, the bakery box sitting on the porch floor gave me a pretty good idea of who it had been, either Gemma or her mother, Marilynn.

I phoned Aaron and ended up leaving a message. So I called 911 and explained the situation. They transferred me to someone who answered the phone "Bomb Squad." I pictured some guy in a tiny office who'd been waiting for weeks to hear the phone ring. Or, maybe hoping it wouldn't.

The first to arrive was the fire truck from Station 5, just about a mile away. I heard their siren from about the time they left the station. I'd gone out the back door, moved my car across the street, and was waiting on the front sidewalk when they pulled up, siren wailing, lights flashing. When I explained the situation and referenced the hotel bombing, that more or less put a damper on their enthusiasm and they pulled the fire rig down the street and waited.

Two police squads arrived a few minutes later. They didn't seem in any rush to check out the box on the porch, either. The police bomb squad arrived shortly after that along with a sergeant who got the two squad cars to move a growing crowd of gawkers back a hundred feet in all directions. The sergeant strolled over to La Grolla, the restaurant across the street and had them evacuate all sorts of folks in the middle of their dinner.

Aaron showed up sometime later. The bomb squad was in the process of suiting up some poor guy who'd drawn the short straw, hanging about a hundred pounds of olive drab protective gear on him.

"Someone pay you a visit?" Aaron asked.

"Yeah, but by the time I made it to the front door, all I caught was a glimpse of the taillights heading up the street?"

"You got any idea what kind of vehicle?"

"Yeah, fast."

"You have any interaction with Mrs. Baker?"

"I told you before, I saw her today, along with her mother. She, Gemma, asked me to meet her at the Tri-Cort Services office with an invoice. I called you after that, and you said not to call you unless I had something good. Well," I said and nodded to indicate the growing crowd, three squad cars, a fire truck, the bomb squad, and the white box on the front porch.

We watched as the guy in all the protective gear was led up the front walk toward the porch. He knelt down behind some armor-plated protective wall with a thick window in it and sandbags piled all around. He began to work a remote control device.

One of the bomb disposal guys walked over and said, "You need to move now, Lieutenant."

We walked behind the bomb disposal truck. There was a guy in the back of the thing monitoring a screen and talking into a headphone I guessed he was probably patched into the poor sucker up near my front porch.

I glanced around and saw a news truck pull in down the block. A cameraman and a woman climbed out and quickly headed toward us.

"Oh shit," Aaron said, looking down the street. Then he focused on me. "You left their office on good terms?"

"Yeah, they offered me cookies. Marilynn, the mother, even let me take the elevator down on my own, said I didn't need an escort. Hell, they cut a check right away and, in fact, added on a hundred buck tip."

"You are *so* buying dinner next time."

Two of the bomb disposal crew jogged to the back of the truck then crammed in around the guy with the headphones. All three were completely focused on the monitor screen.

"That means he's starting to probe. They'll try and get a reading as to what's in there first before they even attempt to move the thing."

"Christ, I should have grabbed my new flatscreen out of the den," I said absently.

Aaron looked at me but didn't say anything.

Another news van pulled up, and two guys unloaded, they spoke to one of the cops at the end of the block then nodded back and forth and started walking toward us. The three bomb squad guys were suddenly in an animated conversation with one another until the guy with the headphones signaled for quiet.

"What's up?" I asked Aaron.

He just shrugged his shoulders and shook his head.

My phone rang a moment later. I was going to ignore it until I saw it was Heidi calling. "Yeah, Heidi."

"I'm watching a breaking news story please tell me that's not your house."

"'Fraid so."

"God, Dev, are you okay?"

"We're just waiting to see what the bomb squad guys come up with."

"Oh my God, I was just over there."

"What?"

"I felt so bad after I blew you off the other night. By the way, I was meeting a girlfriend."

"What are you talking about?"

"When you called, the lecture, green futures."

"Green futures?"

"Hello, anyone home? Yeah, anyway, I was just over there, and you didn't answer the door, so I just left a little treat on your porch. Look, I'm back in my car and heading over right now," she said, and I could hear the alarm on her car begin to beep as she stuck the key in the ignition.

"No, wait," I said, but she'd already hung up.

One of the bomb squad guys looked toward us and said, "Detective," then motioned Aaron over. They seemed to confer about something, then all three of the bomb squad guys nodded in unison, and everyone turned to look at me.

"Get over here, you moron," Aaron said.

I hurried over. The bomb squad guys didn't look too happy, and Aaron was shaking his head. "Dev," he said then, stepped off to the side so I'd be able to get a better view of the monitor screen.

It was a hazy black and white image. I expected to see sticks of dynamite and some fuse mechanism, so I wasn't sure exactly what I was looking at. "Jesus, they hid the thing inside a cake?"

"It is a cake, and that's all it is, a God damn cake for Christ's sake," one of the bomb disposal guys growled. He had a shoulder patch on his uniform, blue background with silver thread that said Bomb Disposal then a wreath thing around what looked like the kind of bomb you'd drop from a plane.

I must have had a blanker than usual look on my face because another of the guys said, "It's a cake, douche bag. God knows why, but someone was just being nice and dropped off a cake on your porch. Hope you enjoy it, probably going to be pretty expensive by the time they add up all the costs involved in getting everyone out here on a false alarm. Not to worry, they'll be sure to send you the bill."

"Let's get the hero undressed," someone said, and then they left to help the guy still up by my porch.

"A cake? Someone is stupid enough to do something nice for you, and you decide it would be a good idea to create a statewide incident?" Aaron asked.

"Statewide?"

"Did you miss the news crews? We'll be sure to mention your name when we tell them it was an idiotic false alarm. What the hell were you thinking?"

"I was thinking about the explosion at the hotel, three people dead, that's what I was thinking."

"A cake, God help us," Aaron said and walked off.

Heidi arrived just as the bomb disposal truck headed down the street. They confiscated the cake she left for me, it turned out to be chocolate, and I figured they'd have the thing devoured in the next fifteen minutes. One of the news vans was still parked down the block, giving what looked like a live broadcast, probably telling everyone in their listening area that I was a complete idiot.

"My God, are you okay?" Heidi asked, then gave me a big hug and a long, hard kiss.

"Yeah, I guess I'll live, but I'm more than a little stressed out."

"I know just the thing for that," she said and flared her eyes as we walked inside, and I locked the door.

The End

Thanks for taking the time to read **Double Trouble**.
If you enjoyed Dev's adventure please tell 2-300 of your closest friends.

Don't miss the following sample of **Yellow Ribbon**.

Sneak Peek

Yellow Ribbon

Second Edition

MIKE FARICY

One

I'd been up with Heidi until almost sunrise. Not a complaint, by the way, more like bragging. Every so often, she gets this insatiable hormonal swing that might last about twenty-four hours. It was incredible—if you could survive. Then, while recovering on my couch at home, I got the call to come over and join the girls. A call? Let's be honest, it was a plea, begging, how could I refuse? It was just that after the previous night of virtually no sleep, I was really running on empty.

I arrived at their town-home late in the afternoon. The rooms had all been painted in the past year. I knew because I'd done the work, then been paid by way of some great dinners. The place was spotless, nice furniture, not necessarily expensive, but nice all the same and certainly not threadbare.

The girls and I settled into the living room. The drapes were pulled, it was very private. At first, we just talked and watched a little TV. Then we ate a simple dinner in the living room, occasionally glancing at the TV, but really just involved in casual conversation and catching up. One thing seemed to lead to another, and now, once I finished the last of my beer, it would be time for me to join them. From where I was sitting, I could hear the laughter.

They'd been in the bathroom for the past twenty minutes chatting away while waiting for me. There were two of them. Sisters. Beautiful. A blonde and a redhead, Emma and Ava. I kept getting them mixed up, I always did, screwing up who was who. Not that they seemed to be bothered. On the contrary, they seemed to think it was kind of funny. They'd both claim to be the other, which didn't help in solving any of my confusion.

"You called me that the last time, I already told you, I'm Emma," the redhead said with a straight face.

"Dev?" the blonde would ask. "How come you always call us by the wrong name?"

Occasionally one of them called out to me from the bathroom and told me to hurry up or asked me when I was going to come in and join them. I remained on the couch, still trying to recharge my batteries from my Heidi marathon.

I finally figured I'd left them alone long enough. I rolled my shoulders a couple of times, then turned my head from side to side, cracking my neck, getting ready to face the music, and not really sure how I was going to handle both of them. I set my empty beer bottle on the living room carpet next to the couch where we'd been playing around earlier. I took a deep breath, steadied myself, and began to head down the hallway approaching the bathroom door with a fair degree of caution.

The door was half open, and as I drew closer, I could hear the two of them in there whispering, giggling, and making plans while sitting in the Jacuzzi. Light from the half dozen scented candles they'd insisted on lighting flickered out the bathroom doorway and into the hall.

"What's taking him so long?"

"I don't know. He's always late."

"He better get here pretty soon."

"Let's splash him when he comes."

"We can hide under the bubbles, and he won't see us."

"Yeah, and then we'll splash him."

That seemed to get them going all over again and they started laughing and splashing one another as I tiptoed toward the door.

"Are you two ready for me?" I called from the hallway.

That brought on squeals of delight, and they both screamed, "Hurry up, Dev. Hurry up."

As I slowly opened the door, I gave a little evil laugh which brought on a series of shrieks, and they slid down in the Jacuzzi beneath about a foot of bubbles until just their heads were exposed.

"You promised you'd get in with us," Emma screamed, or was it Ava? I had them mixed up again, anyway it was the blonde.

"Yeah, Dev, come on, you said you would," the redhead pleaded, then splashed some water and blew a handful of bubbles toward me.

"All I know is, I promised your mom you'd have a bath and be in bed before she got home from her class," I said.

They scooted over to the far side of the Jacuzzi shrieking, and then the two of them started kicking and splashing.

"Come on, now who's gonna be first?" I said and grabbed a thick white towel from the rack on the opposite wall. The floor was already under about a half-inch of water from all their splashing.

"Me, me."

"No, that's not fair let me, it's my turn, you always get to be first, Emma. It's my turn."

"I get to go first because I'm the oldest, and that makes me the boss."

That seemed to click something in my brain, and I repeated, *Emma, oldest, blonde,* to myself a half-dozen times. Then I spread my arms, holding the thick bath towel and shaking it from side to side.

"Okay, now we've got two towels. How about both of you getting out at the same time, and then everyone can be first? How does that sound?"

That brought on more shrieks and giggles as they hurried to climb out over the slippery edge of the Jacuzzi, in the process spilling a couple gallons of water across the white hexagonal tiles of the bathroom floor. A wave of water and bath bubbles washed over my shoes.

"Careful now, we don't want anyone slipping and falling. Take your time, this floor is wet and slippery."

Of course, they completely ignored my wise advice. I threw the towel over blonde, five-year-old Emma's head. Then I reached back and grabbed the towel for Ava. In the process, I lowered my knee, and the leg of my jeans dipped into the water pooled on the bathroom floor. I wrapped the towel around little four-year-old Ava as she stood there shivering.

"Come on now. We'll dry off in your bedroom where it's nice and warm, and then you can both get into jammies."

"I get to pick the story. I know which one to get," Emma shouted and then dashed out of the bathroom.

"No me, it's my turn tonight. Don't pick the one I want, Emma. You can't," little Ava shouted as she started to take off in hot pursuit. She slipped on the floor. Fortunately, I somehow managed to catch her as she fell. She missed the edge of the Jacuzzi with her forehead by just a fraction of an inch. She giggled as I caught her, like her near death-accident was all just a big game. I hoisted her up on my shoulder, and we followed Emma into their bedroom.

"You can't pick my book, Emma," Ava reminded as we stepped into the bedroom.

"I'm going to pick an even better one," Emma said.

"What one? What one are you picking?"

"You can both pick a book, but before we pick books, we need to have pajamas on first."

Who knew slipping a little flannel nightie on could take the better part of ten minutes? Probably most moms, but I sure didn't have a clue. Once the nighties were on, we had to go into the kitchen so they could each have a sip of water. I said no to another cookie, but then decided all three of us could probably do with one, I snuck a second when the girls weren't looking. They picked out their books, said their prayer's including one for me, gave kisses all around, and finally snuggled under the covers.

"Read mine first, read mine," Emma said just as the doorbell rang.

"No me, read mine first," Ava said and then made a face at her sister.

The doorbell rang a second time, and I muttered to myself wondering who it could be as I left the bedroom to answer the door.

A fat guy with dark, curly hair was standing at the door, his back was to me, and he looked like he was scanning the street. My first thought was he must be a neighbor because he was just wearing shirt sleeves, and it was fairly cool for an early October evening. As I opened the door, he turned toward me, a look of shocked surprise washed across his face the moment he saw me.

"Oh, sorry, I was looking for Isabella, does she still live here?" he asked then leaned to the side to look past me and check out the living room.

"Yeah, she does," I said. My initial impression was I didn't like this guy.

"Well then, who the hell are you?"

"Carlos, mommy said you weren't supposed to come back to our house, ever again. You were bad, Carlos, very bad, and you're not supposed to be here," Emma said from somewhere behind me.

I turned to look at a very angry, red-faced Emma just as little Ava peeked out from behind her older sister with a wide-eyed stare. A second later, I saw stars when he blindsided me.

Based on the way my face looked once I came to, he landed a few more punches before he was finished.

The front door was open, the girls were gone, I could only see out of one eye, my lips were swollen, I tasted blood, had one hell of a headache, and Isabella was just pulling up in front.

Two

The paramedic said, "I'd say you have a slight to moderate concussion," I was sitting on the couch, holding a gelled ice pack to the side of my throbbing head. He was kneeling on the floor next to me and in the process of taking a blood pressure cuff off my arm.

As he spoke, he carefully folded the blood pressure cuff and placed it back into a blue case with a red cross on the front.

"At least your nose doesn't seem to be broken, that swelling around the eye should go down in the next thirty-six hours. Maybe keep it iced off and on for the next day or two, and that will help. I'd stay away from spicy foods for the next couple of days with those lips," he laughed. "How's the breathing, any troubles with that nose?"

"You mean can I? Through my nose? Yeah, it'll be okay, I guess. Just trying to clear my head is all, still kind of dizzy, things are spinning a little."

There had to be a half dozen cops in the small townhouse. I could see Isabella at her dining room table occasionally glancing over at me. She was red-eyed, crying, and nodding to some guy in a suit and tie seated across the table from her. He was typing on a notebook of some sort. What looked like a cellphone sat on the table between the two of them, I guessed it was probably recording their conversation. Isabella was nodding, then biting her lower lip. She did not look happy.

It was dark outside, but at least two more police officers were out front, apparently walking back and forth across the front yard with flashlights. A couple of red and blue lights were flashing on top of squad cars out in the street. The lights were shining through the windows, bouncing off the living room walls, and in general, adding to my pounding headache.

"I don't think we'll need to transport you. Well, unless you want us to. But, if I were you, I'd think about going down to the ER and getting checked out. Maybe have somebody drive you down there, preferably tonight. If you don't go down tonight, I'd certainly get in there tomorrow, just to play it safe."

"Thanks," I said, nodding slowly while my head continued to throb, having no intention of going to the ER either tonight or tomorrow.

"I really think you should, sir," he said, reading my mind.

"Appreciate the advice. Mind if I go over and join them at the table. I'm sure they'd like to ask me the same questions a few more times."

"Yeah, sure, we're done here, just take it easy the next couple of days, you got pretty banged up. It looks pretty shitty, but you're awfully lucky, it doesn't seem to be as bad as it looks."

"Thanks for checking me out," I said, then groaned to my feet and took some unsteady steps toward the crowd gathered around the dining room table. I slowly approached, then ran my hand across Isabella's shoulder as I sat down in the chair next to her. She gave my hand a quick squeeze, glanced over at me, and tears immediately started running down her cheeks.

With the mascara and eyeshadow pooled around her eyes, she looked like she'd gone twelve rounds with someone a lot larger than her demure little frame. Her always perfect dark hair seemed limp and bedraggled. There was a pile of Kleenex on the table in front of her, and she held more in her hand.

"Oh, Dev," she said and sniffled when she looked at me then put her hand up to gently touch the side of my face.

I reflexively jerked my head back, which got things really spinning, and I had to grab onto the edge of the table and close my good eye for a long moment until things settled down.

"I'm so sorry," she said and started crying again.

A couple of the uniform cops and the suit at the table looked over at me. My wobbly entrance into the dining room was not exactly the sort of thing that would instill confidence.

"I know you're not at your best, Mr. Haskell. Maybe just rest for a minute or two and think if there's anything else you can add to your previous statement?" the suit said. He looked to be about forty and gave the immediate impression he was not someone to be trifled with. He had dark hair, shaved along the sides up to where a part would normally be, the hair was immediately longer and combed over on the top of his head. He had big, solid-looking hands like he had done labor or maybe farm work early on. He had introduced himself to me earlier, but with all the spinning and the fireworks going off in my head, I couldn't remember his name.

I began to shake my head indicating I didn't want to wait and my skull immediately felt like it was going to explode. I waited a few seconds for the fireworks to stop inside then said, "I don't think I can add anything else, it all happened so fast. It couldn't have been a minute, maybe more like just a few seconds. I don't know what he hit me with, his fists, a bottle, I just don't know. Like I said, I thought he was a neighbor, you know, because he was just in shirt sleeves."

"Mister O'Kelly?"

"Who?"

"Mister O'Kelly, Carlos O'Kelly was the man who assaulted you," The suit looked over at Isabella as she nodded.

"Oh, yeah, sorry, as matter of fact, Emma called him that, Carlos. Said he was bad and wasn't supposed to be here. I turned around to look at her for half a second, and then the lights went out. I didn't know his last name. Like I said, I figured he must have just run over from next door."

"And you were babysitting the little girls?"

"That's right."

"Have you done that before?"

"Yeah, but just once or twice in a pinch," I said, glancing over at Isabella. That started things spinning again, and I took a couple of deep breaths before proceeding. "I've known Isabella since we were in high school. Her husband, Danny, and I were pals. I guess the sitter canceled for tonight." I was going to look over at Isabella but decided to just hold my head still.

"Like I said before," Isabella jumped in. "She called about a half-hour before I was supposed to leave and said she had the flu. That's really the last thing we needed here, flu. So, it was such short notice I couldn't think of who to call, so I called Dev. The girls know him, and he ran right over, it was just going to be for a few hours, not late, it's only a two-hour class. We usually meet for about thirty minutes before class for a coffee and a quick review."

"Where's your husband?"

"Operation Enduring Freedom," she scoffed.

"He's in the service, deployed?"

"No, he's dead," Isabella said.

"Afghanistan, Helmand province, 2011," I added.

"I'm sorry," the suit said.

Isabella nodded and dabbed her eyes again with the Kleenex.

There was a noticeable silence for a couple of beats before one of the uniforms behind me asked, "Do you have a jacket here, Mr. Haskell?"

"My jacket? Yeah, it's a brown leather bomber's jacket. It's hanging up in the front closet."

One of the cops stepped over and pulled the bifold door open on the closet in the entryway. The door was louvered and painted white. It gave a high-pitched squeak as he pulled it open, and the sharp pain in my head seemed to immediately ratchet up with the sound.

"A brown bomber jacket? Doesn't seem to be anything like that hanging in here now."

"It should be on a hanger in there, got a Ranger tab on the left shoulder, it's next to a little pink ski jacket if I remember correctly."

"I see the ski jacket, but there's no brown leather jacket in here."

I thought for half a second, swallowed to keep my stomach down, and said, "My car keys were in there. Can you check and see if my car is out front? It's a black Infiniti QX, two-thousand-five. It's got silver wheel rims, and the taillight on the passenger side is taped over with red tape. There's a crack down the passenger side of the windshield, oh, and a big crease along the passenger side."

The cop stuck his head out the front door then called back in the room, "Did you park it nearby?"

"Are you shitting me? It should be right out front at the curb. I parked it in front of the house," I said, groaning as I slowly got back up on my feet. I had to steady myself on the dining room chair for half a moment.

I worked to keep the contents of my stomach down as I walked to the front door and looked out. There was a police squad with flashing red and blue lights parked exactly where I had left my car. The lights immediately set off a wave of nausea, and I had to close my eyes again until things settled down.

"God damn it, I don't suppose you guys had it towed, did you?" I asked the suit standing right behind me. My question sounded more like I was pleading, hoping they'd moved my car for some reason.

"No, we didn't. You know your license number?"

"Yeah, Minnesota, F-N-L," I said then gave him what I thought was the number. "I'm sorry, I'm still a little foggy, pretty sure the letters are right, but the numbers, I'm not so sure, it's either seven-four-nine or seven-nine-four. I just can't seem to focus too clearly at the moment."

"That's okay, will have it in just a second, you're calling it in, Joey?" he said to the uniform standing next to him and already on the radio attached to his shoulder.

The guy nodded then looked at me. "Haskell, H-A-S-K-E-L-L, first name Devlin. Yeah, two-thousand-five Infiniti QX, black. Did you say there was a rear taillight broken?"

"Yeah, on the passenger side, a crack from top to bottom on the passenger side of the windshield, and then that crease across the passenger side doors."

He nodded, then turned and said something else into his radio, but I couldn't pick up what it was.

"Maybe come back and sit down at the table, Mr. Haskell. I'm sure you're hurting, but we need to get as much information as quickly as we can."

"Not a problem."

"You're a pal of Lieutenant LaZelle's aren't you?"

I was about to nod, but my head was throbbing so hard I didn't dare. "Yeah, we go way back to when we were kids. I was always the better hockey player," I said then gave a throaty groan as I sat down.

"I'll be sure to remind him."

I proceeded to answer questions for the better part of the next hour, but I don't think I was much help.

Three

It was well after midnight. There was an attractive uniformed female officer named Patty Ryan, who had been assigned to spend the night at Isabella's. She arrived maybe an hour earlier and more or less taken charge. She'd picked up glasses and cups from the coffee table, the dining room, all over the kitchen and loaded the dishwasher. She straightened up the kitchen, got the usually spotless living room back into a semblance of order, all the while attending to Isabella and helping her maintain at least a degree of sanity.

Just now, she was making a fresh pot of coffee. Officer Patty and I, along with the other officers, were working to keep Isabella away from the coffee. The paramedics had left some sleep aids, and Isabella had taken one maybe a half-hour ago. She'd been fighting sleep ever since. That sleep aid could kick in anytime now, and it would be just fine with me.

"God, if I'd known he was out there, I never would have left the girls," Isabella said, not for the first time. She had pretty much cried herself out over the past few hours, but that didn't stop her from repeating the same mantra over and over again, blaming herself for something that was clearly out of her control.

"When you told me a while back that your ex-boyfriend was in Pleasant Lake, I thought you meant a house, you know actually on the lake. It never dawned on me he was in rehab."

"Hardly a boyfriend, more like a bad encounter that kept coming back to haunt the three of us. It was one of the conditions of his going back into rehab again instead of the workhouse. They were supposed to inform me of his release at least a week in advance of the date."

"Well, I guess with your new phone number, it looks like that might have fell through the cracks."

"The information we have is that he wasn't released. He just walked away, again, without completing the twenty weeks. Apparently, he's done that before," the detective at the table said.

"Walked out of a rehab facility?" I asked.

"Yeah," Isabella said. "He's done it at least twice that I know of and now this, God. I suppose that means there's a fourth trip to rehab somewhere in his future, plus he'll have to do the workhouse time for the bounced checks."

"I think, under the circumstances, the state might just have a little different plan for his future. I'm sure the girls are all right, he'll come to his senses and bring them home anytime now," I said.

"You really think so?" She sounded like she was grasping at the only straw out there in a very large cesspool of sludge.

"Yeah, we'll have a big welcome home party for them, with two cakes, and we'll invite all their friends," I said, waiting for her to smile. Instead, her lower lip began to tremble, and suddenly, there was another flood of tears. Under the circumstances, who could blame her?

The pounding in my head had gone from being constant to more of a lightning strike mode. Things seemed to be settling down for a moment or two, and then, suddenly this searing pain would race back up my neck and blast across my skull exploding on the right side of my brain like an artillery shell. I made my way over to the refrigerator and exchanged the room temperature gelpack I'd been holding for the cold one I pulled off the freezer shelf.

When I closed the freezer door Officer Patty shot me a look, then walked over and quietly said, "You both should try and get some rest. You're going to have a busy day tomorrow."

"Do you think he'll call?" Isabella asked again.

Officer Patty shook her head and said, "I don't know. I do know that whether or not he calls, we're going to need you, and the girls are especially going to need you, both of you, to be at your very best. Now, you need to get some rest. Don't worry. We're here if your phone rings or someone's at the door, so why don't you just try and close your eyes for a bit."

"I don't think I can," Isabella said.

"You need to try, Is," I said. "I'll flake out on the couch. If anything happens one of us will get you. But, she's right, you've got to be sharp tomorrow, we both do. The girls need you to be at your very best, and you won't be able to do that if you don't get some sleep. So come on, try and close your eyes. We both should."

"I won't be able to sleep."

"Then just rest, but you have to give it a try. You'll be no good tomorrow if you don't try. Come on," I said and then put my arm around her shoulder and guided her down the hallway to her bedroom.

"Are you going to be here in the morning?"

"Yeah, I will be, and then once you're settled, I'm going to help look for the girls. But before any of that happens, you need to get some rest."

"Okay, okay, I'll try. I'm really sorry he did that to you, Dev," she said and indicated my swollen face with a nod of her head.

"Don't worry about it, looks worse than it really is, you've got more than enough on your plate right now."

"Do you think they'll be alright, the girls?"

"They'll be okay. I'm sure Emma is giving him directions right now."

"Oh, God, one time, he yelled and called her a bossy little bitch," she said, and a tear ran down her cheek.

"Don't you worry about that, Is. They'll be fine and probably home sooner than you think. And then we're going to throw the two of them the biggest party you've ever seen."

"I just don't know."

"Well, I do, and like Officer Patty said, you need to get some rest. I'll just be out there on the couch. I'll come get you if anything happens. I promise, so you just lie down and close your eyes. You don't have to sleep, but you do have to try and get some rest, okay?"

"Sorry about your face, you really look like shit."

"You just get some rest," I said.

I closed the door to her room and went back out to the living room. I stretched out on the couch and pulled a leopard skin fleece blanket up over me. I turned onto my left side then cautiously laid the gel pack on the right side of my face and hoped for the best. I closed my eyes, and things started to spin for a moment or two, then settled back down. I drifted off to sleep, hoping a little rest might alleviate some of the pounding and fireworks in my head.

According to the digital clock on the stove, it was just a little after five when I got up and walked into the kitchen. Officer Patty was on an iPad and looked like she was in the process of sending an email. I half leaned over to see if I could get her email address, but the screen had changed.

"Any news?" I half-whispered, afraid even the slightest noise might wake Isabella.

She shook her head. "No, at least not so far. Don't worry. We'll get those girls back safe and sound."

"What an absolute asshole," I half said to myself.

"Yeah, that pretty much sums it up. Based on the list of priors I've seen, he looks like the poster child for spoiled little rich kid. I've seen this kind of history before. It's hard to believe, but he's probably a bigger disappointment to himself than to anyone else. So how's the head?"

"Actually, better, at least the constant pounding seems to have stopped for the moment. Now it seems to be in direct relation to just moving my head too fast. This is just about the worst I've ever had."

"He really nailed you. You're lucky there wasn't more damage, you don't mind me saying, it looks like shit."

"I can't wait to discuss that fact with him."

"No doubt, but if you really intend to help, just let us deal with this butthead, he's not about to see the light of day once we get hold of him. And we will get him. Then, you can visit him and tell him what an idiot he is, but for right now, the best way you can help is by not helping. You should maybe try and get some more rest, it can only improve your condition, and we're going to need you sharp as well as Isabella."

"Hear anything from her room?"

Officer Patty shook her head. "They take about forty minutes or so to kick in, but once those pills from the paramedics start working, she could be out for a few more hours. You wouldn't want to make them a steady diet, but for tonight, under these circumstances, it's just what she needed."

Four

Just as Officer Patty opened the front door and cautioned whoever was out there to be quiet, I came awake on the living room couch. I kept my eyes closed for a moment and listened. I recognized Aaron LaZelle's familiar voice as he stepped into the living room, talking softly and trying not to wake me. We'd known one another since we were kids playing hockey, and I knew the suit who'd been directing the questioning last night reported directly to him. I opened my eyes just as another uniform stepped into the living room right behind Aaron. The uniform was a big guy, and his jacket covered up the name stitched on his uniform shirt.

"No need to pretend you're nice by talking softly," I said and slowly sat up.

"Man, you look like shit," Aaron said.

I smiled.

"Didn't we teach you to duck? So how's the head? How you feeling?"

"I'll make it. You got any news for us?"

He shook his head slightly. "Nothing yet, we got everyone in town looking for your vehicle. We're doing rousts on all known contacts of this Carlos O'Kelly, character. Something will click sooner or later, and things will take off. We just need a little break is all."

I'd heard him give a version of that speech more than a few times in the past. Based on my experience, in reality, what he was saying was, "We are royally screwed for the time being."

"Known associates? You mean barflies, idiots?"

"Yeah, along with family and anyone else we can think of. We're checking everyone and everything, believe me, Dev. I've had teams out rousting folks all night long, and they're not about to stop. Something's bound to turn up, and we'll have those two little girls back just as soon as possible."

"What about the feds?"

"At this stage, I'd prefer not to go there, but we're keeping an eye on that option. The moment it looks like we're losing control, they'll get the call to come in. I don't have any problem with that."

"Do you even have control now? Have you, have we, even for a moment, been in control?"

"Believe me, I understand what you're saying, and I share your frustration, we all do. But this isn't your standard snatch and grab. We haven't heard anything from this idiot, no contact, nothing like a ransom demand, no taunting phone calls, zip. We're still looking at this as a really bad domestic."

"No calls, no contact, what does that tell you?"

"It strongly suggests an impulse reaction. I think if he looks back with some honest, soul searching reflection, he'll start to see the mistakes he's made and find a way to get the girls back to their mother. Then, he'll probably try and hightail it out of town. At which point, we'll grab his ass and lock him up in a dark hole for the rest of his remaining days."

"Honest, soul searching reflection? You got a hell of a lot more faith than I do."

"Faith? No, nothing to do with faith, Dev. Just good hard work that will let us catch a break. That's all we need, one break, Dev. Just one, and then we got this jackass by the short hairs."

I stupidly shook my head, and the pounding suddenly started up again then launched into the fireworks exploding on the right side of my brain.

"You okay?"

"Yeah, just a momentary short in the system," I said.

"There's liable to be another problem, as well," Aaron said after waiting a long moment.

"What's that?"

"Word seems to have gotten out, so the news media is going to be camping on the doorstep here."

"That won't help, Isabella doesn't need all that going on right now. Can't you lock them up or something?"

"We can post someone out front, a squad, at least keep them more or less at bay, if not away. For starters, don't talk to them. Don't give a comment. Don't even let them wish you good luck. Just keep it buttoned up."

"Maybe it would be a good idea if we got Isabella out of here before they show up? You know, so she could avoid them completely."

"No," Aaron said. "First of all, if Carlos plans to phone or somehow make contact, this is the place to be. Secondly, she needs to be here, in surroundings that are familiar to her. And, well, there's still the hope that he might just bring the girls back here. We won't leave her alone. Someone is going to be here with her for the foreseeable future. I'm guessing under the circumstances she's probably had just a couple hours of sleep, fitful at best. How are you doing, by the way?"

"Me? I look a lot worse than I feel at this stage. Sacking out for a bit seemed to help. I get another twenty-four hours under my belt, and I should be back to normal."

"Whatever that is."

I ignored that last comment. "Now, what can I be doing to help?"

Aaron looked at me and shook his head. "Here's what would really help. Please, do absolutely nothing. Please. In fact, the less you do, the better. Well, unless you remember something that slipped your mind last night when Ditter interviewed you. Then we'll want to hear from you, otherwise stay the hell away."

"Ditter, that was the guy's name? I mean, he told me, probably more than once, but I was having trouble focusing, to tell you the truth."

"Yeah, Jack Ditter, he's good, Dev, very good. He's my best, which means you don't have to help. We'll call you if we need you. Okay? So, Have you been checked out?" " Aaron said, changing the subject.

"Me? Yeah, the paramedics were here, they gave me something for the headache. Twenty-four hours will probably be the best thing for me, that and getting those little girls back home safe and sound. Once this swelling goes down, I'll be back to my perfect self."

"You should see a doctor, Dev. Probably a psychiatrist, too, but certainly a doctor just to get checked out and be sure."

"Once those girls are back, I will, I promise."

"I mean this as a friend, Dev we don't want you involved. This is delicate. We're working it the best we can. No one can do a better job, Dev, we've got the resources. So please, do not get involved. You'll only be screwing things up. I hope I'm making myself clear?"

"Yeah, not to worry. I understand, relax, and take a chill pill, man. I plan to stay cool, very cool."

"Please, see that you do."

"I said I would, I promise."

"I'm holding you to that, Dev."

Aaron was still there when Isabella came out of her bedroom. She looked and sounded groggy almost like she'd been drugged, which, upon reflection, I guess was pretty much the case. Officer Patty said her good-byes, told us to hang in there and that she'd be back for the late shift if it was needed. She was relieved by another great looking female uniform, Officer Vang.

"Let's keep it simple. Just call me Tai," she said. Then she proceeded to make a fresh pot of coffee and opened up a box filled with fresh croissants. She placed the box on the dining room table. "My aunt and uncle own a bakery over on University Ave. We all had to work there as kids."

"I thought you cops just ate doughnuts."

She shot a smile at me that was meant to be anything but charming.

Aaron reached in and grabbed a croissant, then took a sip of hot coffee. It dawned on me that he'd been working through the night and was as exhausted as Isabella looked and at least as tired as I felt, he'd had absolutely no sleep and probably no break in the action for the immediate future.

The uniform who had arrived with Aaron removed his jacket, nodded at Isabella and said, "I'm Gary Johnson, I've got a list of people we've been talking to. I'd like you to take a look and see if there might be anyone we've missed, maybe a name that might pop up we hadn't considered or maybe someone we should reconsider."

Aaron sat down at the dining room table and rubbed his face as Johnson handed a two-page list across the table. He looked as tired as Aaron, and I guessed he'd probably been rousting folks out of bed for the past ten hours, not exactly the best way to win a popularity contest.

Isabella quickly ran down the list, then turned to the second page and said, "To tell you the truth, I only recognize a couple of these names. I think this Luci O'Kelly is his grandmother, isn't she?"

"His grandmother?" Johnson said and shot a look at Aaron. "Mrs. O'Kelly is in an assisted living facility, suffering from Alzheimer's. She was unable to be much help. She's his grandmother?"

"Yes, his parents have a nice condo in town somewhere, not sure where actually. I do know they have a home in I think Florida and also in the south of France. God, you don't think he's taken the girls out of the country?"

"No, it would be impossible without passports. The parents, what are their names?" Aaron said.

"The same, Carlos, he's a junior, Carlos the jerk that is, not the father. I think his mother's name is Mary. Virgin Mary, Carlos always called her, a very religious woman, I guess. I've never met her. Like I told them last night, I think he's been estranged from his parents for a while, but his mother sneaks him money from time to time."

Johnson and a couple of the other officers were writing things down.

"The only other name I recognize is this Arthur Goodwin. Isn't he the lawyer who did the plea bargain for Carlos? He had him sent to rehab instead of the workhouse on that last aggravated assault charge, didn't he?"

That's correct. Mr. Goodwin is with the public defender's office and was the court-appointed attorney in the case you mentioned. We'll be talking to him first thing this morning."

I glanced over at the clock on the stove. It was only twenty minutes before seven. If Goodwin had any sense, he was still home in bed.

"Let me give you an update on what we have so far, which isn't much, but that doesn't mean it's necessarily all bad," Aaron said

A cloud seemed to cross over Isabella's face.

"Based on what we've learned up to this point, it would appear the girl's abduction was a spur of the moment incident. It may have been triggered by Mr. Haskell's appearance at the front door, or perhaps your not being home. Right now, we don't know. The positive side of this is that it means this was not a planned undertaking. What that suggests is there is an increased possibility that the girls will be released, possibly sooner rather than later. We are continuing our search and, in fact, redoubling our efforts. We have a statewide BOLO out for Carlos O'Kelly as well as your girls, and just to be on the safe side, we're extending that across a five-state region. I know it's difficult if not near impossible, but the best thing you can do for both yourself and especially for the girls is to remain calm and stay positive until we get them back. And, we will get them back."

Isabella nodded like she accepted the fact they were doing everything possible, which at the moment, other than rousting people out of bed in the middle of the night, wasn't much.

"Let's extend that BOLO to all the states en route to Florida. Find out the address of that Florida residence and contact local authorities and see if we can track down the parents of this idiot," Aaron said.

Isabella got up and walked into her bedroom then came back out a moment later. "I hoped like hell I'd never, ever have to use this again," she said and threw a faded yellow ribbon onto the table.

I'd seen it before. It had been tied to the tree out front when her husband Danny had been deployed. She'd kept it up for a few days after she got the word he'd been killed, but after the funeral, she'd asked me to take it down for her. I'd hoped like hell I'd never ever *see* the thing again.

To be continued....

Well, at no surprise, Dev seems to be in over his head right from the get-go. The city's laziest Private Investigator, Dev Haskell, agreed to help out his friend Isabella and babysit her two young daughters. But, as you can see he's barley on the job and he's already in over his head. You better check out this next book in
the Dev Haskell series **Yellow Ribbon.**

Books by Mike Faricy
Crime Fiction Firsts

A boxset of the first four books in four crime fiction series:

    Russian Roulette; Dev Haskell series
    Welcome; Jack Dillon Dublin Tales series
    Corridor Man; Corridor Man series
    Reduced Ransom! Hot Shot series

The following titles comprise the Dev Haskell series:

    Russian Roulette: Case 1
    Mr. Swirlee: Case 2
    Bite Me: Case 3
    Bombshell: Case 4
    Tutti Frutti: Case 5
    Last Shot: Case 6
    Ting-A-Ling: Case 7
    Crickett: Case 8
    Bulldog: Case 9
    Double Trouble: Case 10
    Yellow Ribbon: Case 11
    Dog Gone: Case 12
    Scam Man: Case 13
    Foiled: Case 14
    What Happens in Vegas… Case 15
    Art Hound: Case 16
    The Office: Case 17

Star Struck: Case 18
International Incident: Case 19
Guest From Hell: Case 20
Art Attack: Case 21
Mystery Man: Case 22
Bow-Wow Rescue: Case 23
Cold Case: Case 24
Cash Up Front: Case 25
Dream House: Case 26
Alley Katz: Case 27
The Big Gamble: Case 28
Bad to the Bone: Case 29
Silencio!: Case 30
Surprise, Surprise: Case 31
Hit & Run: Case 32
Suspect Santa: Case 33
P.I. Apprentice: Case 34
Rebel Without a Clue: Case 35

The following titles are Dev Haskell novellas:
Dollhouse
The Dance
Pixie
Fore!
Twinkle Toes
(*a Dev Haskell short story*)

The following are Dev Haskell Boxsets:
Dev Haskell Boxset 1-3
Dev Haskell Boxset 4-6
Dev Haskell Boxset 7-9
Dev Haskell Boxset 10-12
Dev Haskell Boxset 13-15
Dev Haskell Boxset 16-18
Dev Haskell Boxset 19-21
Dev Haskell Boxset 22-24
Dev Haskell Boxset 25-27
Dev Haskell Boxset 28-30
Dev Haskell Boxset 1-7
Dev Haskell Boxset 8-14
Dev Haskell Boxset 15-19
Dev Haskell Boxset 20-24
Dev Haskell Boxset 25-29

The following titles comprise the Jack Dillon Dublin Tales series:
Welcome
Jack Dillon Dublin Tale 1
Sweet Dreams
Jack Dillon Dublin Tale 2
Mirror Mirror
Jack Dillon Dublin Tale 3
Silver Bullet
Jack Dillon Dublin Tale 4
Fair City Blues
Jack Dillon Dublin Tale 5

Spade Work
Jack Dillon Dublin Tale 6
Madeline Missing
Jack Dillon Dublin Tale 7
Mistaken Identity
Jack Dillon Dublin Tale 8
Picture Perfect
Jack Dillon Dublin Tale 9
Dublin Moon
Jack Dillon Dublin Tale 10
Mystery Woman
Jack Dillon Dublin Tale 11
Second Chance
Jack Dillon Dublin Tale 12
Payback Brother
Jack Dillon Dublin Tale 13
The Heist
Jack Dillon Dublin Tale 14
Jewels To Kill For
Jack Dillon Dublin Tale 15
Retirement Scheme
Jack Dillon Dublin Tale 16
The Collector
Jack Dillon Dublin Tale 17

Jack Dillon Dublin Tales Boxsets:
Jack Dillon Dublin Tales 1-3
Jack Dillon Dublin Tales 4-6
Jack Dillon Dublin Tales 1-5

Jack Dillon Dublin Tales 1-7
Jack Dillon Dublin Tales 6-10

The following titles comprise the Hotshot series;
Reduced Ransom! Second Edition
Finders Keepers! Second Edition
Bankers Hours Second Edition
Chow Down Second Edition
Moonlight Dance Academy Second Edition
Irish Dukes (Fight Card Series)
written under the pseudonym Jack Tunney

The following titles comprise the Corridor Man series:
Corridor Man
Corridor Man 2: Opportunity knocks
Corridor Man 3: The Dungeon
Corridor Man 4: Dead End
Corridor Man 5: Finger
Corridor Man 6: Exit Strategy
Corridor Man 7: Trunk Music
Corridor Man 8: Birthday Boy
Corridor Man 9: Boss Man
Corridor Man 10: Bye Bye Bobby

Corridor Man novellas:
Corridor Man: Valentine
Corridor Man: Auditor
Corridor Man: Howling

Corridor Man: Spa Day

The following are Corridor Man Boxsets:
Corridor Man Boxset 1-3
Corridor Man Boxset 1-5
Corridor Man Boxset 6-9

All books are available on Amazon.com

Thank you!

Contact the author:
- Email: mikefaricyauthor@gmail.com
- Twitter: @Mikefaricybooks
- Facebook: Mike Faricy Author
- Website: http://www.mikefaricybooks.com

Published by

MJF Publishing

Printed in the USA
CPSIA information can be obtained
at www.ICGtesting.com
LVHW011330051023
760085LV00063B/1706